A Patch of Yellow

A Patch of Yellow

Lisa Talbott

Lineage Independent Publishing

Marriottsville, MD

ISBN (paperback): 9781087976273

Publisher: Independently Published by Lineage Independent Publishing, Marriottsville, MD, USA

Maryland Sales and Use Tax Entity: Lineage Independent Publishing, Marriottsville, MD, USA 21104

www.lineage-publishing.com

lineagepublishing@gmail.com

To my parents, who must've wanted to dump us five in someone's barn from time to time... I am forever thankful that they didn't!

Contents

Foreword

This is the second time I have had the honor and privilege of writing a foreword for a Lisa Talbott novel. Her first, "Spud (everything is meant to be)" was released earlier this year. It was preceded by a compilation of her poetry and short stories, "Weep and Wail," with me providing the introductory comments to each section and grouping Lisa's works thematically.

Our trans-oceanic friendship started off when I discovered Lisa's poetry on one of the social media groups for writers that we both belong to. One of her poems was perfect for the novel I was writing at the time. I even held up publication while awaiting Lisa's permission to cite her poem. Overall, our writing journeys are quite similar: self-doubt transformed into confidence, confidence transformed into ambition, and ambition led to publication.

Then there's Lisa's nonagenarian mother, Elizabeth Talbott. She has been a steady influence on both of us as we compose our books. Elizabeth isn't afraid to "tell it like it is" when it comes to the book's content and details. I admire her for her candor.

Writing a book (or a series of books) is no easy task. It takes work. It takes patience. It takes a thick skin during the editing process. It takes dealing with unfamiliar software and technology. Lisa has been through all of that and much, much more. I truly hope that you will find the story she tells in "A Patch of Yellow" enjoyable and engaging. I certainly did!

Michael Paul Hurd
Author/Publisher
Lineage Independent Publishing

Prologue

Lillian sat in silence on the long return journey home, trying to pick off little bits of vomit from her hand-knitted yellow cardigan. It wasn't exactly *her* cardigan, although it was now. It had initially been her mother's, but that was many years ago.

She hadn't had any new clothes for as long as she could remember, save for a dress or two she'd crudely 'run up' on her mother's old Singer treadle sewing machine. But then again, who *did* have new clothes on a regular basis? She had had to make do with her mother's clothes all these years, altered many to fit her, too. Didn't everyone?

And why would she need any fancy new clothes? She didn't go out anywhere; no one to see her in them either, apart from Terry. Terry always told her she looked 'as pretty as a picture' without the need for fancy dresses or lipstick. She would have liked some lipstick, actually; her mother used to wear it apparently. She remembered her father saying that it tasted like strawberry junket. 'What is strawberry junket?' she asked herself.

1

Terry placed his hand over hers, reassuringly, his other on the steering wheel of his truck. He tried to find some words to say that would break the stark silence between them and justify what they'd just done. To sanctify the stomach-churning fear and guilt, the over-whelming loss he knew he was going to have to acknowledge and live with their actions.

He couldn't chastise either of them. Certainly not his Lilly, it would never have been her idea.

But it *was* for the best. The best for Lillian; for the children; and especially for him.

******

Chapter 1: February 1946

Boo was barking and running round and round in circles, resembling a Rottweiler, possessed. Why on earth she was acting like that was mind-blowing for Emma.

Boo was a four-year-old Border Collie; didn't have a vicious or aggressive bone in her lithe canine body. The most proficient and agile sheepdog they'd ever owned - but the most fearful of even her own shadow! When the planes soared overhead, Boo would scramble fitfully, trying to get where water couldn't! She had an aversion to certain songs too, wind-chimes and music. There was a beautiful old piano in the corner of the living room which Emma could only play when Boo was out with Ted in the fields, gathering in the sheep. On an evening when she would deign to play, Boo would throw back her head and howl! Singing 'Happy Birthday' was totally forbidden in their homestead because the hound obviously hated it! Scratching relentlessly at the hearth rug, trying to get underneath. Emma despaired of her.

It was gone eight-thirty pm. All the sheep had been fed and penned up for the night. Ted had also called it a day and was stacking up the range, adding more and more wood. He'd had three ewes that had lambed that afternoon and it had been an exhausting day. He'd already lost one lamb and when Emma went into the barn to take him his mid-afternoon cup of tea, she stood in the doorway, holding back, watching her beloved man's shoulders shake as he sobbed, cradling the stillborn lamb in his big, strong arms.

It was all par for the course with sheep farming - you win some – you lose some, but every loss was a huge tragedy to Emma and Ted. They loved all their animals, foolishly naming each one. It was Mary who had lost her lamb, her second loss.

Boo would not be pacified, which was not unlike her. She scratched at the back door, anxiously. Frankie, the white cat who professed to be deaf though his act didn't fool everyone, raised his head, turning to watch Boo, then lay back and curled up once more on top of Emma's bag of knitting wools.

Emma decided she had to pacify Boo and opened the door. She flew down to the barn where she continued running round and round in circles. It is the nature of a

Border Collie to herd, needing every 'family' member to be together and Emma couldn't decide if Boo's antics meant that a sheep had inadvertently been forgotten and left outside, or that a predator of some kind, was lurking. This was, after all, a vexing time, with the war just ended. People were still desperate – and hungry.

There was no way a sheep had been left outside though, Ted would never have misplaced any one of them, neither would Boo! And this concerned Emma.

Boo scratched at the barn door and Emma had no alternative but to open it and follow her inside. The dog quietened, becoming subdued, whimpering as she stealthily searched around ... then flattened herself on the barn floor, looking up at Emma with her tongue hanging out, and sighed. Mission accomplished!

Emma walked back into the kitchen with Boo inches from her heels and stood behind Ted - still at the range - waiting for him to acknowledge her so she could enlighten him as to the reason for Boo's peculiar behaviour. At the sound of a baby's whimper, Ted turned around.

There was a brief hesitation in his statement as he observed his wife and the bundle in her arms. Emma's expression of total bewilderment mirrored his own. "What ...?" his confusion expanding even further when he noticed a toddler hiding behind her!

"Ted," she whispered, "they were in the barn!"

Chapter 2: The Foundlings

Ted wiped his blackened hands up and down the side of his trousers, staring at the surreal sight before him, at a loss as to what to think or say! The baby in his wife's arms was becoming more vocal and started to wail, the toddler hiding behind her stood rigid and silent, his unnaturally pale face devoid of any expression.

"Ted, what are we going to do?" Emma asked, beseechingly.

A question Ted struggled to find an answer to. His mind was doing somersaults, his heart palpitating and resonating in his ears. Who were these children? Where did they come from? Where were their parents? How had they come to be in the barn? What were they doing in his kitchen, with his wife?

It was almost nine p.m. The children must be petrified. They needed to be fed, tucked up in a warm bed, safe at home, and Ted was keenly aware that he and Emma needed to reach out to someone, but who?

They calculated the boy must be about three years old, and the baby? Well, just that – a baby; possibly six to nine months old? They'd never been blessed with children, so they were out of their depth.

Ted squatted in front of the little boy. "Hello, Sonny, what's your name?" The child edged further back, hiding behind Emma. "Ha, a little shy, are we? Well, that's ok Sonny, that's ok. And this little bundle of joy here, is it your brother or is it your sister?"

Emma looked at the bundle in her arms for any tell-tale sign, trying to decide if it was a he or she. There wasn't, the baby only had on a terry towelling nappy, but was wrapped in the most exquisite hand-knitted shawl, in an off-white Shetland wool. Expensive wool, too, Emma noted. She'd never been able to source, nor afford, Shetland wool!

Ted judged from Emma's facial expression that the baby was in desperate need of a nappy change, and milk, according to the screams being emitted.

Emma glanced back at the toddler standing behind her, and she took his hand, gently explaining to him that she was going to tend to the baby, get some milk ready, and told him not to worry, reassuring him that everything was going to be all right.

Trefellon was a charming and quaint little abode, a typical Welsh homestead constructed from enormous boulders and surrounded by acre upon acre of rolling countryside. Ted had inherited the cottage and land after the untimely passing of his parents and was named accordingly after horrendous storms battered the little village of Aberdovey one dreadful Easter Sunday night. The rains had been torrential and the gales unrelentless. The old Yew tree was swaying rhythmically with the force of the wind, and it eventually came crashing down on the cottage, shattering the little bedroom window, but miraculously not causing any other structural damage. Hence the name Tree Fell On (Trefellon).

The middle-aged Welsh couple had little means to feed a baby. They'd rarely had visitors at all during the war years. The occasional supplier, of course, and the butcher who came periodically to take the sheep to the abattoir for slaughter and distribution but being self-sufficient eliminated the need to make frequent lengthy trips to the markets. They grew all their own vegetables, they kept chickens, bantams, and rabbits. Sunday morning church service attendances were a rarity with neither of them being devoutly religious.

If the baby had been nursed by the mother there was no chance of anything like that now; they only had cows' milk, and not a great amount of that! Emma panicked: they were shepherds, used to looking after animals, not children. What were they going to do? The infant continued to wail, louder and louder.

She lay the screaming, kicking bundle on their kitchen table, gently removing the shawl and the soaking, ammonia-stinking, soiled nappy. As she undid the nappy pin and carefully removed the fabric, she gasped in horror, covering her mouth with her hands. The skin from the little girl's bottom came away, stuck to the terry towelling, the red-raw flesh shining like a hot coal ember. She suddenly felt conscious of what her reaction must portray to the little brother who had stood in silence, beside her, so she hurriedly altered her whole demeanour; smiling, and humming the tune to 'Rock-a-bye baby' and hoping the little fella was familiar with it.

"Wock-a-bye Marley on the twee top . . "

Emma and Ted looked in surprise at the pale-faced little boy who was gazing adoringly at his screaming sister as he reached over and held her little white hand. He turned to look at them and said softly, "she cannae talk yet."

Miraculously, Marley's screams subsided a decibel or two. The evident familiarity of her brother's intervention had been a comfort, a welcome distraction from the present.

"So, this is baby Marley?" enquired Ted, "your baby sister. I'm Ted and this lady here is my wife, Emma. What's your name again, Sonny?"

The child looked at the appraising, waiting faces and turned back to his sister. "She's hungry."

"Are *you* hungry, Sonny? Would you like a bowl of porridge?"

He still didn't react, never releasing his sister's hand or moving from her side.

Emma looked over at Ted with a sense of urgency as he went to the pine dresser taking down a bowl, cups, and salt. He put a saucepan of water on the range and congratulated himself for stoking up the fire, only an hour earlier. He'd make some porridge for the boy and boil some milk for the baby. Marley. That's what the youngster had said her name was, Marley. A name he'd never come across before: now he needed to find out who the little fella is.

Chapter 3: First Night at Trefellon

Emma joined Ted, who was drinking his mug of tea, sitting in front of the range, Boo lying at his feet. It was still deliciously warm from all the wood Ted had piled on earlier. She looked at him, waiting for him to tell her that it had all been a figment of their imagination: a huge joke.

She looked around at their little kitchen; the table where she'd cleaned the baby, the empty bowl from the little boy's porridge, the soiled nappy that she would have to boil in the morning because she didn't have any more to dress her with. She'd had to cut up an old hand towel and use that as a makeshift nappy! She'd rubbed some Vaseline on the baby's sores. She didn't know what else she could've done. She remembered an old wives' tale of mixing Robin Starch and applying that to the baby's bottom, but the wounds were raw and she was doubtful she ought to do that. Vaseline was the best alternative she could think of administering at that time of night. She thought she may have some 'Jack-by-the-hedge' in the garden (*also known as poor man's mustard*) which was not only a fabulous additive to salads, but wonderful for treating cuts, wounds, ulcers, etc; though she wasn't too sure it was out, yet. She'd have a look in the pantry later, to see if she had any poultice left over.

"What are those two babies doing in our barn, Emma? Where have they come from?"

Emma wanted to laugh! They'd had the most challenging day with the birthing of the lambs, and now they had two *real* babies thrown into their laps. There was nothing more they could have done tonight other than feed them, change them, and put them in a bed.

"We'll have to do something in the morning, Ted. We'll have to inform someone. Somebody must know who they are." Ted nodded.

"That little girl. She's just a mite, poor thing. And the boy, oh Ted, that poor little boy."

Ted had made the boy a bowl of porridge, which he was very reluctant to eat – at first, it wasn't until he saw his sister taking to the bottle, that he decided to pick up his spoon, and eat.

Emma had used one of the bottles she used to feed the lambs who wouldn't or couldn't feed from their mother, for the baby Marley. She'd placed the bottle and teat into a saucepan of water and boiled it, ensuring everything was adequately sterile to use for a small baby. It was just warm milk with a teaspoon of sugar added.

Ted still hadn't uttered a word. "We'll notify the police tomorrow. There must be someone who will recognise these children. They can't stay here..."

"*Why* not?" Ted cut in, rather abruptly. "Why in God's name not, Em! Somebody doesn't want them, that's evident, isn't it? Someone just dumped those little mites in our barn! *Dumped* them, Emma! No note, no one knocking on our door asking if we'd be kind enough to mind them for an hour or so while they did whatever they needed doing! Dumped them like disposable garbage, they did. And at night-time too. Yes, they can stay here, Emma, they bloody well *can*. They can stay here until we find out the reason *WHY* they're here and what their story is!"

Emma was quite taken aback! It certainly wasn't like Ted to raise his voice. In fact she'd rarely heard him be so vocal or passionate about anything... well, for a long time.

Ted would have made a wonderful dad. He'd always wanted, dreamed of having a big family with lots of children running around Trefellon. It hadn't happened in his younger days, he being an only child and losing both his parents to Cholera in 1910 when he was just thirteen years old.

Cholera had been devastating, decades earlier, claiming fifty-two thousand lives in Wales alone. It had rarely raised its ugly head after the pandemic but isolated cases did infrequently occur and when his mother started to complain of leg cramps – 'restless legs' she called it - no one considered what it might be . . but she was restless, and irritable. Her thirst could not be quenched, and she was always having to 'nip out the back'.

His father fell foul shortly afterwards and Ted, just reaching adolescence, found himself having to witness complete strangers bathe his parents' bodies in bleach, blocking up all their orifices, then placing them in body bags to prevent further contamination before being interred into their graves.

Trefellon needed to breathe new life. It *needed* children to run around the surrounding acres and Ted was desperate to achieve this. What was the point in living if he couldn't pass on his love and his knowledge to someone who felt like he did?

He dared to envisage an opportunity now, with these children. He and Emma could raise them and teach them everything about sheep farming. No one would know or question their arrival, would they? They could claim they were evacuees who were still waiting for their families to come forward, or distant relatives perhaps. His mind was inventing all kinds of scenarios to keep them. It was God's gift to them after all these childless years. It was meant to be.

"Emma. I don't know why these kiddies have ended up in our barn. I don't understand how anyone could do that, just leave them with complete strangers. But did you notice the boy had an accent? When he said 'she cannae talk yet' and 'she's hungry', he said 'cannae' not can't, and 'hongry'; they can't be from around here. Em, let's leave it be, for now. Let's wait and see if their parents come back, we don't want to get them in any kind of trouble, do we? Chances are the parents will come back in the morning and explain everything, so no harm done, hey?"

Emma listened, and smiled. How could she refuse this man? Of course he made sense in everything he was saying. He always did. He had so much empathy for everyone and everything. And who could say what the story was about the parentage of these babies? Like Ted said, "chances are the parents will come back in the morning and explain everything."

Hmm, thought Emma, not as forgiving as her husband; what kind of person would even think of discarding them like this, in the stark, unforgiving darkness with no love nor comfort?

An evil person, she concluded. "A cruel, heartless, unfeeling monster."

Chapter 4: Realisation

Ted was an early riser. He'd always been an early riser, taking advantage of the daylight hours and retiring early at night-time, thus avoiding the use of candles or paraffin for the lamps. There was livestock to attend to, chickens to be fed, pens to be mucked out, land to be worked, more ewes would be lambing and now two extra little mouths to feed.

The clock on his bedside cabinet told him it was three-fifty am, not yet time to rise but he was already wide awake, his thoughts immediately returning to the events of the night before. He gently pushed back the gold satin eiderdown, consciously trying not to wake Emma, but he needn't have been so considerate as she immediately stirred. "Ted, what's wrong? Are the children okay?"

"I'm awake now Em, I'm just going to have a peep."

"I'm coming with you."

Emma had removed the contents of one the drawers from the chest-of-drawers in the little bedroom next door to theirs and put the baby inside, placing it beside the little boy who she'd put in the single iron-framed bed. She'd managed to find an old blouse of hers and used this as a nightgown for him. It buried him, his pale, skinny little body lost inside.

The bedroom door had been left ajar and the couple stood in the doorway, peering down at the two sleeping babes, both of them snuggled together in the *drawer*.

"A beautiful sight indeed," said Ted, grinning.

It *was* a beautiful sight, thought Emma, and oh how more beautiful it would be if they *could* keep them, but of course it was unthinkable, someone would eventually come and apologise and take them away and she knew that Ted would be sorry to lose them. She'd listened to him talking last night, she felt the excitement emanating from him as he was describing scenarios of how they could keep them at Trefellon. She'd watched his face light up when the little boy eventually tucked into his bowl of porridge that her husband had lovingly made for him.

It would mean so much for them both to be able to be parents, to shower their love on these little beings who had been placed – for whatever reason - in their capable hands. Had God answered their prayers at last? Only time would tell.

"Cup of tea, love?" he asked Emma. She nodded, yawning. It's going to be an interesting day, she decided; she had two children to feed, she had work to do with the animals, she felt the equilibrium of their secular world shift, and she liked it.

Ted took up the poker and raked around in the range, ash and embers falling in the grate. He added more wood and filled the brass kettle with water, putting it atop the hob. Boo had been lying by the hearth and was happy to find one of her masters pouring water into her bowl.

Emma emptied two heaped spoons of tea leaves into the China tea pot, waiting for the kettle to boil. Ted was sitting at the pine table, his dressing gown hanging loose over his pyjamas.

He was a handsome man, Emma's husband: she'd always considered herself a very fortunate woman, thanking her lucky stars endlessly. He was kind, compassionate, and an adoring partner. He had a mass of dark curls that were

beginning to recede, and long black eyelashes that she
envied. Standing over six feet tall he towered above
Emma, her being only five feet five. She was petite, a
strawberry blonde. Not a raving beauty, she knew only too
well, and that's why she felt lucky; Ted was a great catch.

"The little ones may wake soon, being as though they're in
strange surroundings. Love, I want us . . , no, *need* us to
talk about this. I want us both to be united in this."

The kettle steamed, Emma poured the boiling water into
the tea pot, put the tea cosy on, and sat down in front of
Ted, listening as he continued.

"Like I said last night, I think it's best we wait and see what
happens, you know, in case the parents come back. In the
meantime, they've been entrusted into our care, and I
take that as a huge compliment. I'd like us to do our best
and enjoy what time we're allowed with them. Nobody
else knows they're here; if anyone comes round and asks
questions, we'll decide on what answers we will give. I
have a cousin somewhere up north I could say the kiddies
are relatives that we're looking after. What do you think?

Evacuees or relatives? Emma, we must be in complete agreement. If you feel we should notify the police I don't think I will be too happy with that. That little lad looks as wishy-washy as a wet Sunday. Doesn't look like he's spent much time out-doors. I feel that you and I have been given a chance, Love… I think what I'm trying to say is that I'd really like us look after them for now, and… well, what do you think?"

Ted's voice wavered, he was emotional and Emma didn't know how to reply. She, too, felt like it was a blessing bestowed on them but at the end of the day these children must have a family somewhere? She was under no illusion that at some point someone would come knocking on their door and take them away, just as easily as they had come and left them in their barn!

"Ted, you wonderful old softie, of course I'm in agreement. For however long we're privileged to parent them then that's exactly what we'll do. Like you said, it will be an honour." She placed her hand on top of his, smiling; a pact was made.

Their conversation, however, was interrupted by a creaking floorboard, above them. They looked at each other, realising that movement was happening upstairs. Ted was the first to remove his hand, he leapt up from his chair and headed towards the staircase. There, standing at the top of the narrow wooden staircase holding on to the banister, in a wet nightgown, was the pale face of a very bewildered little boy.

Ted sprinted up towards him, "Hey, Sonny, good morning." He picked him up in his big, strong arms, cradling him as he made their descent. "It's all right Sunshine, come downstairs and have a cup of tea with us. Is your sister still asleep?"

The boy stared at Ted but offered no reply. "Em, get a shawl or a blanket, the boy's cold." Ted sat him on a chair with them at the kitchen table. The boy looked forlorn. He'd wet himself; Ted knew that but wasn't about to mention it. He winked at Emma, "hope you have another blouse you don't want."

Emma wrapped a crocheted blanket around his shoulders before pouring out a cup of tea for him. He was, again, reluctant to pick it up and drink so Ted picked up his own drink, put it to his lips and made a big slurping sound, smacking his lips afterwards. Et voila: the boy chuckled!

24

The first emotion he'd displayed, and a positive emotion, too. Ted and Emma laughed. The boy continued giggling, picked up his cup of tea and mimicked Ted, slurping his drink, until all three laughed and laughed. A breakthrough, at last.

Boo left her position at the hearth, not wanting to be left out of the shenanigans and put her front paw on the boy's lap, her face turned towards his. "Hello, bonny lass."

Ted and Emma chuckled. "That's our Boo, our top employee, she helps me gather all the sheep together. She's a good girl," Ted said, patting Boo on the top of her head, then slowly continued, "do you want to tell Boo who you are?"

"Where's Mammy?"

The couple looked at the boy, then Emma replied "your mummy has had to go away for a while so she asked us if you and Marley could stay here, with us, just until she's able to sort some things out. It will be like a little holiday for you, for all of us! Ted and I are really happy that she chose us for you both to come and stay with. Silly me and Ted though, we forgot your names, but it doesn't matter because we remembered Marley's name so I'm sure we'll remember yours soon."

"When you've finished your cup of tea, Son, we'll all go back to bed and have another hour or two's sleep and when you hear the 'cock-a-doodle-doo', you'll know that it's time for some breakfast, unless that baby sister of yours wakes everyone up before the cockerel," Ted added, light-heartedly.

After everyone had finished their cup of tea Emma changed the boy's wet nightgown. She had shown him the chamber pot she kept under the single bed before she tucked the two of them up only hours ago, but he wouldn't use it. She couldn't possibly have taken him to use the outside thunderbox before he went to bed, it was too dark; daunting for adults to walk the thirty yards in the dark let alone a frightened child!

She was about to change his bed and put on some clean, dry sheets when saw him step into the drawer and curl up next to his baby sister.

Chapter 5: Emma

Emma was born a Cardiff girl. A 'city girl' it was claimed; Cardiff being the capital of Wales. She felt nothing of a 'city girl', and certainly not a 'Cardiff girl'! She hated Cardiff with a vengeance and all the horrendous memories it encompassed. Not that she ever told a soul – other than those who knew already, who couldn't NOT have known. She'd never breathed a word to Ted, he was too nice for the truth to be told. It wouldn't have mattered anyway, it had happened. T'was all in the past. Swept up under the proverbial carpet like unwanted dust.

It was 1915, she was sixteen. The world was at war, and she was working in the administrative department of the Health Department, along with two of her long-term girlfriends, Karen and Lynne. It was Saturday night, and a local theatrical group was going to perform a couple of short comical plays in the village hall and three local sisters would also be there, doing their dancing/singing recitals - everyone was going to be there.

Emma, and her twin sister Jennifer, had been excited about the upcoming event, for days. They were looking forward to being able to wear their best dresses and shoes in readiness for the local lads who had not yet been 'called-up'. They were going to enjoy the night and let the trials and tribulations of the world's current situation pass them by.

They arrived at the village hall which was bedecked in bunting; red, white and blue. Streamers in every corner of the room, the stage adorned with the necessary props and equipment for the entertainers.

His name was Hugh. Considered to be the heartthrob of Cardiff, simply because he was the lead actor of the theatrical group. And he wasn't the only one who considered he was the heartthrob of Cardiff, Jennifer did too.

Emma couldn't quite see the attraction although she did acknowledge his obvious charisma. He was confident and good-looking. His blue-black hair and his crooked smile were very alluring and when he sang *"There's a little spark of love still burning"* by Henry Burr, he accomplished all he'd set out to. Couples leaning in closer to each other would feel that tap on their shoulders, warning them of becoming too close!

During the interval, many retreated to the crisp outdoor air for a cigarette and to exchange thoughts and opinions about the night's entertainment, congregating at the entrance, and whilst Emma, Karen and Lynne chatted enthusiastically they were joined by three young men.

A million times over she would live to regret the night because as she politely bade goodnight to her kindly 'admirer', Hugh leapt from the stage and ran over to her. He caught her arm, turning her round to face the huge, big grin on his face.

She looked around furtively for her sister, Jennifer, she spotted her, glaring at her! She hoped Jennifer would come over and intervene, claim her crush, but Hugh - now with his arm over Emma's shoulder - was leading her outside, along with the many others who had gathered there.

Emma had never considered herself the prettier of the sisters. In fact, she found fault with every minute detail about herself. Her eyes were too small whereas Jennifer had big, wide, smiley eyes. Jennifer was vivacious whereas Emma wasn't, she was quieter, more studious. Jennifer was curvy; Emma was skinny. It was evident they were sisters, but hardly anyone would realise they were twins.

The air raid sirens suddenly blasted out a piercing shrill and everyone started screaming; scrambling for the safety and security of the air-raid shelters. Everyone apart from Hugh, who was in no hurry to join them, running in a totally different direction. As the adrenalin took over, he thuggishly threw Emma to the ground and pushed her dress up to her waist, he unbuttoned his trousers, biting her neck, totally ignoring her screams that went unheard as the overhead enemy planes squealed above, dropping their cargo of bombs on the village hall that had minutes before been filled with music, laughter, and a sense of oblivion to the outside horrors of life as they knew it.

Three remaining singing quartet members and eight young courting couples never made it outside that night, and one innocent girl also lost something very precious - too precious to be taken without consent, and so hideously.

Six weeks later Emma sat at her desk at the Health Department typing up hospital notes on her Imperial typewriter. The J key had locked with the E and she was trying to realign them when Karen walked over, placing a cup of tea on her desk, "I think that one day typewriters will become obsolete, replaced with something much quicker and easier to use."

Emma looked up at her colleague, with contempt, "Sure, and that's the day that you and I will be unemployed. Kaz, don't talk nonsense, of course typewriters won't ever become obsolete. How else is anything going to get written up, published, distributed? How are reports going to be produced, or books and newspapers? Typewriters will never be obsolete."

Karen tilted her head towards the cup of tea she'd left on Emma's desk, "whatever. Drink it while it's hot."

With inky fingers Emma grabbed her cup, took it to her lips and took a big gulp - when the smell hit her - spitting the whole lot over a morning's work of type-written notes! "Urgh! The milk's off," she screeched!

Karen looked daggers at her, sniffing her own cup and taking a sip, studiously analysing, "no it isn't. It's fine!"

Emma covered her mouth. "I'm gonna be sick, that milk...", she ran from the office, desperately trying to reach the toilets in time but it was too late, vomit projected from her mouth, running through her fingers and splashing onto the corridor floor.

She stood over the sink in the ladies' toilets, studying her pallid reflection in the mirror. She felt very queasy and had a dreaded fear that she did not want to acknowledge. She ran the water tap, splashing her face with the icy cold water and sipping some from the palms of her hands. She went into one of the cubicles and sat on the toilet seat, never bothering to close the door, and as she sat there, her forehead perspiring, trying to calculate her last period, her head fell on her knees... and she wept.

"Please God, no. Please, please, please NO!"

She was sixteen. Sixteen years old. She'd only started having her periods twelve months ago, a late starter, she couldn't possibly be pregnant! What would everyone think about her? She'd be a wanton floozy, 'good to the lads' folk would say, and what if they were right? Had she led

Hugh on? No, she most definitely had not! It was her sister that was keen on him, not her! He'd forced himself on her and it was vile.

Jennifer reacted furiously with Emma when they were both back at home, throwing unfound accusations at her, demanding to know where the pair of them had been, when noticeably they'd not been in the air raid shelter with everyone else. She was totally oblivious to Emma's distress, and Emma could not bring herself to explain the real reason for their absence when she doubted she would have been believed. Her sister would have wrongly assumed that she and Hugh had had nothing more than a romantic interlude, wishing it had been her who he chose. Emma wished it had been Jennifer he chose, too, not that she would have wished that sick indignation she had just endured on her or anyone. The man was a vile pig and his crime – because that's exactly what it was – destroyed the sisters' once-solid relationship and she vowed not to tell a single soul.

Karen's grandmother was going to the cemetery on Tuesday afternoon. She went every fortnight to lay flowers on her family's graves; a brother who didn't live to see his first birthday, two sisters, another brother and her parents who all succumbed to the Cholera pandemic, the very one that wiped out those thousands, decades earlier.

"The house will be empty," Karen told Emma, "I know what to do, I've seen my Gran do it loads of times for girls in your situation. I've sterilised the knitting needles."

Chapter 6: The First Morning

"I want to see my baby. Where is she? I want my baby NOW!" Emma tossed and turned, "let me see her, where is she? Bring her to me, she needs me! Help me somebody, please . . help me . . ."

"Emma! Emma, Love. What's wrong? You're okay, it's okay. The baby's still fast asleep but I doubt she will be for very long," Ted chuckled. "Are you okay Em? Shall I bring her to you? Stay there, Love, stay there and I'll fetch her."

Their moment was interrupted by a cry, reminiscent of the vixen who continually frequented Trefellon during mating season, stealthily circling the chicken coops. Of course, it was Marley, hungry again for her bottle.

Ted stood at the side of their bed, his six-foot, semi-dressed stature lovingly cradling the crying, kicking infant. His face, not filled with dread or abhorrence, but with pure devotion. He was smiling and muttering sweet nothings to her as though she was able to understand his every word.

"Here you go Mother," he said, handing Marley over to Emma, "I guess it's over to you now."

Emma apprehensively reached up to take her, whilst wondering how they were going to do this, what they were going to feed her. Ted would have to go into town and buy some supplies, the baby would need more nappies and baby-formula, but she worried that the town folk would become suspicious as to why they needed these unusual items. She knew she had milk and was sure that baby formula consisted of just cows' milk, wheat and malt flour, and potassium bicarbonate, all of which she had; she even had a can of Carnation Evaporated milk. She'd look through one of their encyclopaedias to reassure herself of the correct ingredients. She had another couple of old towels she could cut up and use as nappies in the interim, and she needed to check on the child's sores!

The one thing they need have no worry over was eggs, they always had an abundant supply, she would coddle one; the boy could have his scrambled. Well, she satisfied herself, thankfully she had breakfast covered.

And then another thought hit her like a ton of bricks, and she gasped! She would have to spend all her time with the children. She wouldn't be able to help Ted a fraction as she had always done. Looking after two infants was going to be a full-time job and Ted was going to have to manage on his own until...

A pram, too, she thought. Marley would need to be put outside in the fresh air at some point, she'd need something to *be* in. Oh my goodness, so many things to think about. They really were totally out of their comfort zone.

"Well little Miss Marley, it's a good job you're too young to know what's happening but your big brother will know, won't he? I bet he misses his mum, poor little chap. And we don't even know his name yet, do we? Do *you* know? We can't keep calling him Sonny can we?" and then Emma smiled at the sound of the name Ted had fondly used. "Hmm, Sonny?" she repeated, "actually that sounds quite nice. I like it. And don't you worry about your mummy and daddy, I'm sure they'll be back soon."

Ted had gone downstairs and already had the kettle on the range, eggs and milk on the table, bowls, cups and cutlery. The little boy had also risen, he'd followed Ted downstairs and was sitting at the table, his little legs swinging from his chair. As soon as he saw Emma with his sister, he scrambled down and ran towards her. Marley smiled at him as he took hold of her hand.

"She certainly loves her big brother, doesn't she?" Ted said. The boy didn't answer. "I believe Marley would like eggs for her breakfast, Sonny. Would you like some scrambled eggs for your breakfast, too?" Still no reply. "Boo's going to have some eggs and so am I. They make you big and strong," he said, emphasising the word 'strong'.

Emma placed Marley on a blanket, on the floor. She took an egg coddler from the dresser and grabbed a little saucepan. She poured some of the hot water from the kettle into the saucepan in preparation for coddling. Ted was beating half a dozen eggs in a bowl to scramble. Everything was ready within minutes and the adults felt relief to see 'Sonny' clearly making light work of the food put before him.

Marley was now on Emma's lap, her little mouth opening like a baby bird waiting for its mother to feed it. It was a satisfying moment, watching them eat with such enthusiasm! Ted and Emma ate very slowly, relishing the moment.

"I think Boo and I are going to need a bit of help today, feeding the chickens and rabbits. Would you like to come with us, and see the animals?"

Surprisingly, he nodded!

'Sonny' only had the clothes he was wearing the night of their arrival at Trefellon and they were in a pitiful state. Marley had none. Emma would have to do something to clothe them somehow but struggled to find a solution. What *was* that mother thinking of, leaving the two of them without a stitch to call their own? She found herself getting angry with the 'mother'. *She* wouldn't forsake one of her rabbits or chickens the same way this woman had done with her children. Not so much as a by your leave - disgusting.

She felt she would have to make them some clothes, but when on earth was she going to find time to do that? She already needed to boil nappies in readiness for the 'next time', change the boy's bed clothes that he'd wet and wash his underwear. Talk about being thrown in at the deep end; Emma was slowly but surely beginning to realise the actual depth of their situation, considering that maybe they ought to seek help after all?

The kiddies had no toys to play with, no cot for the baby, and no justifiable reason for them to be there! "Oh Ted," she murmured, "God help us."

"This is Nora, that's Dora, and that white one over there is Clara," said Ted, pointing out the chickens. "Ah, and this is little Dotty here, she's loves her dust baths," he said chuckling, "Chloe, Mabel, Muriel and Lilly."

"Lilly," echoed the boy.

"It is," humoured Ted, "would you like to give Lilly some food for her breakfast? then we'll let them all out to have a run around. They like to be outside so they can scratch around in the dirt."

Ted let 'Sonny' put his hand in the bucket of grain which he released on top of Lilly's head. The chickens started to cluck, running around, fleeing from their coop. Ted would return after feeding the rest of the animals, to collect the eggs.

They next walked over to the rabbit hutches. There were twelve hutches, two rows - six on top of six.

"Now *here* we have a different situation, 'Sonny'. The rabbits aren't allowed out, they'd run off into the meadows and wouldn't come back home. The chickens are different you see; they always like to come home to roost. They *like* being tucked up in their own beds at night, just like we do.

I'll open the latches and you just put a bit of food on the floor for them. Oh look at Billy, he's ready for something to eat. That's right, just there so he can get it."

"Billy," he uttered, smiling.

"You're getting to know them all already. I can see that you're a real clever boy, 'Sonny'."

"Billy," he said again, pointing to his chest.

"Wha . . . What 'Sonny?'. Billy? Are you Billy, too? Is that your name?" The boy nodded.

"Heey, Billy! Now that is a grand name for a good boy like you. Billy. Ahh, well Billy, then I shall address you by your lovely name. Oh I may forget from time to time and still call you 'Sonny', but that's just a term of endearment, and of course you won't understand what a 'term of endearment' is either, so Billy it is! Come on then Billy, you've the sheep to meet. Boo, come along now."

With his oversized blouse swamping his tiny form swaying with his footsteps, his boot laces untied, Billy followed Ted to the sheep pen, a slight purpose in his stride.

Bronwyn was on her back and grinding her teeth noisily, a sure sign she was in pain. Ted hurried over to her, endeavouring to move her onto her side which was the normal position for the lambing labour process, the water bag already evident. He chastised himself for not being in the pen earlier and noticing.

He felt the environmental situation wasn't appropriate for young Billy, so he walked him back to the house, explaining to Emma what was happening in the sheep pen. Emma wanted to rush out to the pen to help Bronwyn, to comfort her, but her maternal ministrations were needed elsewhere, now.

Oh dear, poor Bronwyn. Emma felt her dilemma but this sheep was a veteran mother who had produced two lambs last year and one who wouldn't be seeing another Spring after this lambing season was over. Once she'd finished nursing, she was on the list for the abattoir, along with others.

Chapter 7: Eiffion

It had been six whole weeks since their lives were disrupted and turned completely upside down; they were exhausted. Emma had occasionally found herself justifying the children's mother's decision to resort to such drastic measures, then hastily chastised herself for even daring the thoughts to enter her mind. If it *had* actually been the mother or the parents. Who knew who were responsible for abandoning these children?

Her thoughts were not justifiable of course, but she hadn't experienced going through a pregnancy, giving birth then gradually enjoying been weaned into motherhood. It was hard work for both of them, and no doubt more so for little Billy who was still wetting the bed, despite being put on the potty every night.

He'd asked for his 'mammy' a few times and all Emma could do was reiterate that 'she was having to sort out some problems' and tried to reassure him.

In between the naps the children had, Emma had set to on her sewing machine making items of clothing for them both. A little pair of dungarees and a tunic for Billy, a cotton and lace dress for Marley, the cotton salvaged from a torn and worn sheet that she'd edged with the lace she had left over from making her wedding dress. She had started to knit Ted a jumper, then unpicked it all and made a jumper for Billy instead, miles too big but he'd grow into it. It was nothing as luxurious or elaborate as the Shetland wool shawl Marley had been wrapped in, but it was serviceable.

It was now seven months since the war had ended and the men had begun to graduate home, though some still hadn't made it back; those still recuperating in hospitals, and some not wanting to return to the life they previously lived. One, it was rumoured, fell in love in France, forsaking his heartbroken fiancée, back in Aberdovey.

Ted would arrive back at Trefellon after a trip into the town, relaying to Emma stories of things he'd heard from the men there. The men he'd seen with missing limbs, facial disfigurements, those rejoicing and those seemingly afraid of their own shadows.

He had mixed feelings about his inability to relate to these brave war heroes. He respected and admired wholeheartedly those who had gone and given their all "for King and Country" but couldn't decide on whether he felt lucky to have been spared their experience, or shame that he wasn't allowed to have participated.

Farmers were exempt from conscription and as the war progressed, they were requested and expected to produce more and more with fewer and fewer labour resources. Emma had contributed as much as Ted throughout. They'd once had a local lad who came over every day to assist with the planting, animal feeding, fence building, until one day he simply hadn't shown up, he'd gone - forged his mother's signature it was told - and enlisted. He was fifteen years old, his name was Jim: youngest son of Frank and Nellie Perkins. Nellie's husband Frank, their two older sons, and Jim, never returned to Aberdovey. Neither did any of their three compulsory-purchased horses.

Nellie wasn't exactly the most 'admirable' woman, so the talk went. She was formidable and ruled her roost with an iron rod, her menfolk nothing like her! The local gossip was that Nellie, in her younger days, was quite accommodating to anyone who looked her way, and apparently poor innocent Frank had done more than that! Well and truly snared, she and Frank had produced three wonderful, grounded, and handsome young men. So wonderful, in fact, that all three readily went off to do their duty, in unison. Young Jim had been left behind to do his mother's bidding until he'd gathered enough bravado to follow in his father's and brothers' footsteps. Whilst Aberdovey mourned the loss of these fine gentlemen, few felt any sympathy for Nellie's feigned grief.

It was eleven a.m. and Ted had had a busy morning! One of the rams he'd been shearing had slipped from his grasp and the clipper had cut into its belly - not too deeply it looked – although the blood travelled horizontally between his back legs. He'd have to administer a poultice before the flies got inside. Many a lamb, sheep and ram had been lost over the years due to maggots feeding from them. He needed to get them all sheared and dipped in time for the summer, which seemed to be approaching faster than any year previously.

Emma's assistance was missed tremendously! Everything to do with the farm was now resting on Ted's shoulders and he knew he would need to recruit some help imminently, but he also knew he would be putting the children at risk: they'd be talked about and folk would start asking questions as to why they were there. They'd both been adamant they wouldn't subject themselves or the children to suspicious scrutiny, so it daunted them as to how best to approach the situation.

Eiffion Rhys was a rebellious Aberdovey boy who had upped sticks and moved to Edinburgh in 1935, four years before the war broke out. He resembled nothing of a traditional Welshman. Wales did not pull at his heartstrings like the majority of his patriotic kinfolk.

Eiffion didn't even care for his God given Christian name, insisting everyone called him Ivan. He was camp, vivacious, theatrical, flamboyant, and extremely comical. Everything was a huge joke to Ivan and he flaunted his extremisms wherever he laid his head. Yes, he'd been to war and yes, he had endured the most horrendous ridicule, taunts and jibes. He cared not a single jot, he loved himself and if anyone couldn't find that fact alone appealing, that was their problem – certainly not his.

He adored being at war, surrounded by so many virile, strong and admirable men. He entertained them all, in more ways than one! Very few would have considered Ivan a hero, until they encountered it with their own eyes.

When he first arrived in Edinburgh four weeks after leaving his hometown (yes, he walked!) he was painfully thin! The soles of his boots had worn away, his beard was long, and he stunk like a polecat! He had but a few coppers in his pocket which he would not deem to spend until he was absolutely desperate! He encountered a drinking trough for horses, outside a drinking establishment in the Grassmarket and he knew he was at the Grassmarket when he encountered the statue of Greyfriar's Bobby. He leapt inside the trough, fully clothed, savouring the feeling of cold water on his parched and filthy body, his garments squelching as he thrashed about. He sat there for about ten minutes before taking out his cut-throat razor and giving himself a much-needed shave, taking years off his persona. He climbed out and hurriedly tried to find a shelter or somewhere he could dry out, sleep, and anticipate his future years in Scotland.

Indeed, Ivan had found his niche in Scotland. He was reborn; he *was* most definitely Ivan now, not Eiffion. He walked around Princes Street drinking in every detail, he danced through Princes Street Gardens eyeing the castle, visualising himself in a Black Watch tartan kilt dancing the Highland Fling. Oh, it definitely had to be a solo dance, he needed to be the star of every show.

And for the next two years he achieved everything he set out to accomplish, well - almost! The men who he aimed to bestow all his love and affection on were none too eager to reciprocate. A huge population of Scots were miners and were 'afeared' of 'Nancy-boys'. A true Scotsman was entitled to wear a skirt, but 'dinnae mock its history'! Ivan, many a night, endured a kicking and a beating - just for being 'him'.

When the war broke out and men were being called up, Ivan was reluctant to join in, considering the option of claiming himself a 'conscientious objector', which wasn't a lie. He hated violence. Goodness, he'd suffered enough horrendous violence throughout his life, he would never dream of inflicting harm to another person or being. He knew only too well the long-lasting effects sticks and stones left on a person. And then he remembered a baby rabbit that had appeared before him whilst on his long walk from Wales to Scotland. The rabbit just sat there - and he hadn't eaten for two days.

Desperate times, desperate measures. It would be cowardly of him to refuse to join the men who were prepared to leave everything behind them. Their wives, children, families, their scruples and beliefs. So... he too went to war.

Effion... Ivan... bumped into Ted whilst Ted was counting out what money he had left over after buying their supplies. He'd seen some rope in the hardware shop and thought he'd purchase several yards. No-one would be suspicious of buying rope! It could be for a number of uses, but Ted had decided to make a swing for the boy, Billy. The Yew tree had been gone decades before, but there was a perfectly placed apple tree at the side of the cottage with a strong overhanging branch where he could place this rope, to construct a swing.

He turned to go back to the hardware shop to buy the rope and almost bumped into Eiffion (as he knew him by), causing both of them to grasp each other's arms.

"Eiffion, oh I'm so sorry, son, forgive me for not looking where I'm going," said Ted, berating himself the second he noticed his missing leg.

"Mr Talbert," Ivan acknowledged, in his theatrical way "tis I who do not have a leg to stand on for being in your way! I am but an encumbrance and it is my very self who should proffer apologies to your good self."

Ted could not restrain himself and he burst out laughing. He and Emma had known Eiffion since he was a young lad and everyone from around there knew he was 'different' but this was the first time that Ted had actually had a one-to-one confrontation.

"Eiffion, it's good . . .

"Ivan, please. Eiffion was stifling for me. I'm Ivan now. Oh, I know what the people round here call me. 'Ivan the

Terrible', 'Eiffion the dicey-en', the 'queer fella', and no doubt they'll conjure up another amusing nickname to satisfy their morbid sense of humour . . Anyway, likewise, Mr Talbert it's good to see you again, I assume that's what you were about to say, before I interrupted you?"

"Ivan! Yes, that is exactly what I was going to say," said Ted, chuckling and smiling from ear to ear. "And Ivan," he continued, emphasising his name, "you wouldn't perchance be looking for a bit of work, would you? The missus and I have been looking for a one-legged, discrete, humorous man to help on our farm. We've been a bit stretched, you could say, lately. Got a barn you could sleep in. That IS of course, *if* you were looking for something."

"Mr Talbert! Discretion is my middle name. Seven-thirty tomorrow morning, ok? Oh, and by the way, I do trust the lovely Mrs T has some Earl Grey in her cupboards?"

Chapter 8: The New Hand

True to his word, Ivan arrived at Trefellon the following morning at just before seven thirty a.m. Ted was amazed to see that he had walked all the way on his crutch, a journey that took him ten minutes in his truck! He cringed with embarrassment at his failure to understand how Ivan would manage to get to the farm.

Emma had been relieved to learn that Ted had actually managed to procure some help around the place, daunted at the prospect of the disability of the said help, concerned about their secret being maintained, and who on earth was Earl Grey? She'd never heard of him, let alone tea being grown in Great Britain! She kept tea in her tea caddy, the sort that could be bought from the town, like every other housewife in Wales.

Billy was sitting at the kitchen table eating a boiled egg and Marley was now crawling around on the wooden floor. Emma had pleaded with Ted to invest in some linoleum covering that was becoming all the latest trend but he'd explained it was an unnecessary expense that they could do without; they would just have to hope that Marley didn't get splinters in her knees! Ivan had knocked on the door which Ted had opened and invited him inside to join them for breakfast and a cup of tea before beginning the daily chores.

"Woah, Mr and Mrs T! I didn't know you'd finally got around to having a family."

Emma looked panic-stricken at Ted. "Ah, yes, well, this is where we're relying on your discretion; it's a very long story. Do you take sugar in your tea?"

Ivan tilted his head, a teasing grin on his face, if this was going to be dramatic, he was going to be all ears. He placed his crutch next to a vacant chair and sat down.

Ted took his time as he relayed the story to Ivan, all the time consciously choosing his words so as not to cause any duress to Billy, who kept looking from face to face to gauge the gist of the conversation.

"So, Billy, you and your little sister are going to be spending time here, and helping feed the animals, too, I understand?" Billy nodded.

"How old ARE you Billy?"

"Four," he replied.

Emma and Ted looked exasperatedly at each other. They hadn't thought to ask him how old he was!

"Four? That's a wonderful age. And you've come all the way from Scotland."

"Scotland?" exclaimed Emma and Ted in unison.

"You didn't know? Didn't you detect his accent?" They both shook their heads.

"I did notice an accent, yes, but never dreamt they'd come from as far as Scotland! I just assumed they weren't from around these parts," explained Ted.

"I spent some years there, just before the war. Going to go back again, I hope! Beautiful country. Not dissimilar to Wales but on a much grander scale. I wanted to be on the stage, theatre; dancing, singing. Ah well, some German sniper put paid to my dancing career," he said, tapping the stump of his missing leg, "but not my ambitions. I plan on returning one day and opening up my very own establishment. Mr T, Wales was never very kind to me, or my ilk, and that's why I wanted to leave, get away and reinvent myself. When I've got myself together, I am going to create a safe haven for entertainers; those who, like me, want nothing more than to play to an audience. I've got it all planned up here," he said, tapping his head.

Ted, Emma and Billy, sat entranced.

"Right, well now, sitting here blabbering all morning won't get the baby a new bonnet. Are you going to show me around, tell me how I can be of service?"

"Just one more thing, Ivan," Emma jumped in, "we don't want to get anyone in any kind of trouble; you know . . . " she winked, hoping he would understand.

Ivan did. "Mrs T. God works in mysterious ways. Seems to me he knew exactly what he was doing *here*." He hung his head, contemplating for a second or two. "Mr. T... walk with me outside. I've had a thought."

The two men rose, leaving the table and Emma; their day was just beginning.

Billy had finished his breakfast and he was anxious to run upstairs to get dressed and join the two men outside. It had become his responsibility for letting the chickens out of the coop and collecting their eggs in the mornings; a task he felt incredibly privileged to be entrusted. He didn't want anyone trespassing on his territory!

In the weeks he'd been at the farm, he'd learned all the chickens' names off by heart. He was learning to count too and every morning he'd run back inside shouting out the number of eggs he'd collected. He was just as valuable an employee as Boo; that's what he'd been told.

And he'd definitely started to look a whole lot healthier. His previous pale complexion was now rosy and he'd plumped up a little. His hair was red which against his previous lily-white skin, had looked carrot-coloured. Now, with being outside more often, his colouring had altered, freckles had appeared over his nose and he glowed, his hair being more of a deep rust hue. It was just then that Emma realised that yes, he did actually *look* like a Scot!

"Mr T. First off, I want to thank you for giving me this opportunity . . ." Ted tried to interrupt, dismissively, but Ivan held up his hand, continuing. "No, please. Not many folk around here are like you and your dear wife. You've always been a decent chap, Mr T." Ted smiled, letting him continue and enjoying the praise. "And what the two of you are doing now, with these children, well . . . it's admirable. I can one hundred percent understand your wish to keep it all quiet - gossip can be such an ugly pastime. Anyway, as I was saying, I think I might have a loophole, your answer, so to speak."

Ted waited: his eyebrows raised.

"A fella I knew who lived in West Lothian, in Scotland, was killed during the war. His widow was so overcome with grief, worried about how she was going to cope with two youngsters, etc, she went into depression and took her own life. No one to look after the children so yours truly asked you and the lovely Mrs T if you would be willing to help out, until such time, that is, as alternative arrangements could be made? What do you think? We could elaborate more if necessary."

Ted pondered what he'd just said. That would be a solution in the interim, they'd both feel more comfortable with that version rather than the dirty truth! And then when the real family came back and claimed them, no-one would be any the wiser.

A smile spread across Ted's face; it was a nice little scenario. He wouldn't feel the dread of going into town and asking for anything out of the ordinary. He felt sure that their neighbours would be accommodating and sympathetic. They'd probably bring over some toys, or clothes.

"I wonder if they've been registered." Ivan thought out loud. And that was a question Ted hadn't even considered!

"Anyway, I have brought along my meagre belongings and I will kip down in your barn as you kindly offered, so lead on and show me what I have to do."

It was a decent enough barn and in good condition, not too small to feel claustrophobic and not too large to get lost in. Eiffion... Ivan... had never been used to luxury anyway and was more than happy to consider it his temporary home. Ted had cleared an area of animal feed and added a few bits of old furniture: a tallboy for his personal possessions, a single wooden bed with a straw mattress, a feather pillow, a few sheets, and a blanket for the cold nights. Emma left an earthenware water bottle for him to fill with hot water, in readiness for the winter.

She felt guilty offering Ivan such humble surroundings, but Ted suggested that their barn would feel like a hotel considering the years of sleeping under the stars during his war stint. "Certainly no bed or feather pillows for comfort then," Ted reminded her.

"Ahh," Ivan sighed when he walked through the barndoor, "home sweet home."

Chapter 9: Marley's Birthday Plans

The swing was up and Ted and Ivan couldn't conceal their excitement, calling for Emma to come outside and pat them on the back for all their efforts. They'd both taken it in turns to have a go, ensuring the bough was strong enough to support their weight, giggling like a couple of schoolboys while Billy looked on, patiently waiting for his turn.

Emma was up to her elbows in flour and lard, she'd been making the pastry for the meat and potato pie for the night's supper. She stood in the doorway watching the two adults fooling about and her first thoughts of anger dissipated as she observed the three of them, viewing each one's heartaches through new eyes.

There was her beloved husband whose dreams of becoming a father had never been fulfilled. Young Ivan, who had endured years of pain from taunts and bullying simply for being someone who others considered 'not normal', the horrors he undoubtedly encountered at war and losing his leg, and little innocent Billy who hadn't got a clue as to why he was there instead of with his family and the fact that he stood there, with the older men, made Emma realise exactly what a blessing the scene she was witnessing, was.

She wiped her hands on her apron and hurried over, picking Billy up and sitting him on the swing, positioning each of his hands on the ropes. She then gradually pushed him, slowly, slowly, his face beamed, and he too started to laugh.

Emma had completely forgotten about Marley who was now crawling about as fast as lightning. She'd started to cut her teeth and as well as being cranky, her face was often flushed. Obviously hearing the hilarities outside, she'd crawled towards them and Billy was the first to notice her. His immediate response was to put his arms out to reach her, letting go of the ropes and in doing so toppled backwards, his head hitting the earth ground. His smiling face instantly turned into a grimace of pain and Emma frantically grabbed hold of the still-swaying seat. Ted hurriedly picked him up and noticed a little trickle of blood running down the back of his head, he strode indoors, needing to bathe it - everyone followed.

He sat him atop the kitchen table while he got a bowl of water and some cotton wool, silent tears wet his cheeks. Billy stared at him. "I'm sorry," he whispered.

"Billy, there's no need for you to apologise, you've done nothing wrong, lad," Ted reassured him, "it was just a little accident. We'll wash you up and have this fixed in two shakes of a lamb's tail."

Billy knew this meant he would be fine again in seconds as he'd seen how quickly the lambs wagged their tails.

"Is he going to die after it d'yer think Mr T?" asked Ivan, winking at Emma.

"Well, he didn't die before it, so I guess you might be right, but look how brave and resilient he is, Ivan. Reckon you could have done with lads as brave and strong as our Billy here, when you went off to that war."

The so-called humour was lost, of course, on a child of his age, but those words 'is he going to die after it' would worry him for ever! He couldn't understand why everyone was laughing.

For all of Ivan's showmanship, comedic banter, disability, he had definitely – so far - proved to be one of Ted's better acquisitions, a breath of fresh air to have around the place.

Every morning he joined them at the breakfast table. He insisted on washing himself at the water pump outside, never at the kitchen sink. He knuckled down and worked without stopping until Emma would call them in for something to eat. He was neither intrusive nor abusive.

Billy had taken an instant liking to him and followed him around like a shadow, to the point of ignoring Boo. With Billy, it was now 'Ivan this,' or 'Ivan that,' and Ted was beginning to feel a little jealous! He'd still insist on Ted tucking him up in bed every night and standing outside the 'thunderbox' on a dark evening before he went to bed, but during the daytime, it was Ivan he sought out.

Ivan never stopped talking or singing to him. If he was fixing a fence and needed one or two more nails, he only had to ask Billy to fetch some and off he'd run to ask Ted where he could find them and then he'd run back, just like an obedient dog!

It was Friday night and Emma and Ted lay in their bed, reading. "Ted, Marley has now got six teeth, she's starting to pull herself up against the furniture and stand, tottering for a while."

Ted took off his reading glasses, turning to his wife as she continued. "Well, I think she must be coming up to a year old."

A year old? He contemplated that statement. All these weeks and weeks had passed and they'd heard nothing from the parents. He truly did believe everything had been a mistake; a spur of the moment decision, that they'd reconsider and come back offering profound apologies, thanks, and explanations. But no, nothing.

Ivan had been right. His suggestion that the children's parents were 'friends' of his who needed short-term guardians for them was perfect. The villagers were now aware and had been empathetic towards them, bringing them bundles of clothes and toys. One kindly neighbour had visited with her own toddler, a daughter – Patricia - the same development size as Marley, the same red hair, but entirely different temperaments!

Marley could easily have been mistaken as Emma's natural daughter. Emma was a strawberry blonde and Marley's hair was a light red, and when people began to point out how much she looked like Emma, she felt a huge shift in her feelings. She began to develop an overwhelming feeling of *love* towards her and felt that this was her only chance of becoming a 'mother'.

"I want her to have a birthday party." There, she'd said it!

She turned to face him, not having dared to before her declaration. "I want to make an official statement, Ted. The children should be able to live as normally as possible and a birthday party would be the perfect opportunity. Billy would be overjoyed. I bet he doesn't even know when his birthday is, and I think the time is right to do this now and tell him that his birthday is coming up soon, and we'll do the same thing for him. What do you think? Shall we ask Ivan's opinion about it in the morning?"

"No we will not!" retorted Ted. "We will *not* ask his opinion, Em, because we don't need anyone's opinion, that is a bloody brilliant suggestion!"

He jumped out of bed, laughing like Emma had told him the funniest thing he'd ever heard.

"Em, get your dressing gown on. Go and wake Billy and take him downstairs, I'm going to the barn to wake Ivan."

"Ted! It's ten o'clock at night!"

"And I don't care if it's the middle of whenever because you, my darling wife, are a genius and I bloody love you!"

And so it was. Marley's first birthday was going to be celebrated at Trefellon on Saturday, 18 May 1946, and a few people from the village were going to be invited. Billy had told Ivan he was four years old, so Emma was determined that he too would have a birthday party, but that Marley's was before his.

He'd been fast asleep when Emma roused him from his bed, asking him to come downstairs because she had a secret to tell him. He understood what a secret was, he'd heard that word before, but he didn't know what a birthday was, or what a birthday party was.

He sat at the kitchen table listening to the adults making plans about cakes, bunting, tables laid, jellies. He watched them smiling and laughing and thought it must be a nice thing they were doing, for Marley.

"Ivan, can I sleep wi' you in the barn tonight?"

Chapter 10: Ted

'Ivan, can I sleep wi' you in the barn tonight?

Those words reverberated in Ted's ears and pierced his heart with a force more powerful than any German sniper's bullet to Ivan's leg could have done. He was gutted and ashamed at feeling so. Of course Ivan was going to fare more of a father figure than he, who was old enough to be his grandfather, it was natural. Nevertheless, it had rankled.

He lay in bed that night with the back of his head resting in the palms of his hands on his pillow staring at the ceiling, going over the last few years, then further beyond.

He shouldn't be doing this, he told himself, he needed to sleep; he had to rise early to attend to all the animals. Villagers depended on him and the farm and it was *now* that was important, not the past.

Some things were like that, though. It was easier said than done to let sleeping dogs lie and forget everything. But memories never lie dormant or vanish forever, they keep popping up for no particular reason whatsoever other than to remind us that sometimes they're good, sometimes not so. It could be a certain smell, a song, a taste even. And sometimes it could be a few words not dissimilar to *'Ivan, can I sleep wi' you in the barn tonight?'*

He had no idea of how old he was other than that he'd woken during the night, he'd had a bad dream. He dreamt he was standing on a chair in the kitchen, wearing only his nightshirt. There was a wolf there but he couldn't understand where the wolf had come from or what it was doing in his house, but the wolf stalked him, circling, then jumped onto his shoulders and bit off his head! He woke up in a panic, sweat running down his back and that's when he tiptoed into his parents' bedroom and tapped his father on his forehead, "Daddy, can I sleep with you tonight?"

His father didn't stir, but his mother had heard him and she beckoned him over to her side, pulling back the bedclothes so he could snuggle up next to her.

When he woke in the morning, he thought he had probably wet the bed because his feet felt sticky, but warm. He put his head under the covers, not understanding why the sheets and his mother's nightdress were red with blood. He hadn't understood his parents' explanation of the word 'miscarriage'.

With both his parents taken by Cholera and he being just a teenager, Ted felt he was carrying the weight of the whole world on his shoulders. The entire future of Trefellon rested with him and he hadn't even had sufficient time to mourn. It had petrified him having to watch his mother and father be prepared for their graves in that way, their nakedness he'd never seen before, and it had haunted him ever since.

His father, Clifford, had been a good dad and a good teacher, though he often struggled to recall images of either of his parents, now. They'd never owned a camera so photographs were few and far between. He had only a handful of their wedding photographs taken in 1896, their expressionless faces eternalised in sepia, that never saw the light of day, remaining forgotten and untouched, at the back of the bureau drawer.

He did recall fond memories of his mother though, before he was called upon to help his father with the farm work.

He remembered how his mother would include him with baking cakes, asking him to break the eggs and drop them into the bowl while she stood poised ready to mix. He remembered being given the empty bowl to lick afterwards which he thought was the sweetest taste in the world.

And then he remembered the day his father had summoned him to the sheep pen to watch how to slaughter the sheep, his father declaring he was old enough to assist. Ted thought he would *never* be old enough or capable of doing what his father had to do.

It was a ewe that had never been able to get pregnant and therefore, not a viable commodity. His father was going to slaughter it and send to a neighbouring farmer in exchange for a young ram. Ted was told to hold her head while his father slit her throat. He fled the sheep pen, screaming, his clothing covered with the splatters of blood!

He'd never ever been able to do that to a single one of his flock, that's why he always arranged for the butcher to come to their farm. That incident was engraved in his memory and he had vowed he would never participate or witness anything like that ever again. He wouldn't kill the chickens or the rabbits, the task always went to the same man.

Ted bumped into Emma in the autumn of 1917; literally, he bumped into her, she was eighteen and he was twenty. Emma had moved from Cardiff, wanting a fresh start, so she'd chosen Aberdovey which was far enough away from prying eyes and malicious gossip, and a twin sister she no longer had loving feelings for.

She was heading to the post office to enquire for potential work; he was coming out of the post office after depositing two shillings into his post office savings account. She was furious he hadn't been looking where he was going; he was laughing as he caught her before she faltered.

They had a simple wedding twelve months later, neither of them wanting a huge affair and a lot of fuss. She made her own wedding dress which caused her many a sleepless night. She could not get the seams right and ended up having to unpick darts and seams time and time again, eventually having to wash the whole thing before the big day as it was decidedly 'grubby' by the end of completion, blaming every fault on the sewing machine, which very nearly ended up as fire fodder!

Ted assumed the natural progression would be that a child would come along imminently, but his hopes seemed to dwindle as year by year, the good Lord appeared to pass them by.

The sudden arrival of Billy and Marley had delighted Ted more than he could imagine and he began to selfishly hope the parents would never come back to claim them. Naturally, it meant a lot of work for Emma and for him too as Emma wasn't able to help out with the farm work now, but he knew the children would be better off at Trefellon, they were already looking much healthier, and so his thoughts returned to Ivan.

Grow up Ted, you silly old fool, he chastised himself, the more people that love them the better, and Ivan *did* love them. The planned birthday party for Marley would be a big milestone, it gave them structure, normality.

Chapter 11: The Birthday Party

It had been a tremendously busy week at the farm for everyone! Emma had actually gone into town with Ted to hand out invitations to a few children to Marley's party, leaving their children with Ivan for an hour or two. She'd gone to the shops to buy candles to put on the birthday cake, jelly mixes and blancmange to make a trifle, balloons to hang outside, and some apple-green ribbon to adorn the birthday girl's party dress she'd made.

It was Saturday afternoon; Ted and Ivan had ensured all the animals were fed and their jobs attended to before knuckling down to trim up the kitchen in readiness for their guests. Patricia was coming and so was Mandy, Carolyn, Martin and Benjamin. Carolyn and Benjamin were older, more Billy's age but Emma conceded it was a good age mix as Billy needed friends too, and she felt it important that Billy was given leverage to the festivities nominating him in charge of ensuring everyone was issued a party hat upon arrival.

It was a good move because – as always - he took his task to heart, seemingly to have grown a couple of inches taller that afternoon. He actually greeted their guests with a broad smile and a party hat in his hand.

He'd been terribly excited over the last few days, standing on a chair at the kitchen table keenly watching everything Emma was doing. Dipping his fingers in the cake mix, helping Ted and Ivan blow up the balloons, (he even put a party hat on Boo who just lay there, content to allow him to do so).

And indeed the party had been a great success, the children thoroughly enjoyed themselves and the icing on the cake was just that – the cake! They'd played the games; passing-the-parcel, blind man's buff, pinning the donkey's tail, and now the candles were alight on the cake, singing along to 'happy birthday to you' as Boo began her inevitable howling and Marley clapping her chubby little hands, when suddenly there was a light rapping at the door.

Everybody turned to see the woman in the doorway. The children totally disinterested - turned back to look at the cake that Emma was just about to cut up.

"Jennifer!" exclaimed Emma.

Jennifer took in the scene before her and screwed her face up in surprise. "Erm, am I just in time for a little piece of that birthday cake?"

Emma put down the knife and walked over to give her sister an obligatory hug. "Everybody, this is Jennifer, my sister." Then, whispering, "Jen, I didn't know you were coming."

Jennifer looked all around at all the faces, the children, her confusion evident and Ivan grinned from ear to ear, knowing she was going to be in for a real treat!

Ted walked over and gave Jennifer a warm embrace and a peck on the cheek, "cup of tea, Jen? We've got a lot of catching up to do, great to see you again."

Emma finished cutting up the birthday cake, the children shovelled it into their mouths, the mothers - realising the party was over - quickly gathering up their offspring and everybody left.

"Well," said Jennifer joining everyone at the kitchen table, "this all looks very cosy. I came here to tell you my news but I'll let you go first, can't wait to hear your excuse why you didn't bother to tell me that I am auntie and that I have a niece and nephew." She took out a packet of cigarettes and lighter from her handbag, asking for an ashtray, and lit up, not bothering to ask if anyone minded!

"This is Billy, and this is Marley. It's her birthday today," said Emma.

"Mmm," said Jennifer, blowing out smoke, "she looks like you."

Ivan realised that Emma and her sister needed to be alone, to talk, so he picked up his crutch and rose from his seat. "Jennifer, it has been an absolute pleasure to make your acquaintance. I will leave you two lovely ladies to chat while Billy and I go and take Boo for a run outside. Come along Billy, girlie chats can be so boring for us men. Boo, come along."

Bless Ivan. Always knowing what to say, what to do and what not to do or say. And so Emma told Jennifer the story.

"Wow! Well that tops my news by a hundred miles. You're not going to keep them are you, what if the parents come back? Have you notified anyone? Em, you can't just keep someone else's children just because you *found* them in your barn!"

"Yes, we can, that's exactly what we are doing!" bellowed Ted, "we're giving these kiddies love. We're parenting them, welcoming them into our home. We don't know what kind of life they had before they came to be here because I'm telling you Jen these children were in a very sorry state when we found them, and while they *are* here, Emma and I are going to do our utmost to make sure they stay safe and well looked after."

"Jen," Emma continued "the war's over. Maybe their father was killed and the mother couldn't cope with two youngsters on her own. Lord above everyone suffered but perhaps she didn't have any support, anyone she could turn to? We don't know; we don't know anything about them or their past, but we do know that over the last several weeks both Ted and I, and Ivan, have seen a big improvement. In both of them. Poor Billy wouldn't utter a word at first. He wet the bed every night. He helped me with Marley. Ted and I feel responsible for these children and we feel we've all been given a second chance. We're determined we're not going to give them up. They're ours now. Our son and our daughter."

Jennifer raised her eyebrows and her hands as if in submission, "good luck sister, you might have told me though. I would have come bearing gifts."

The ice was broken, everyone chuckled. "And now it's your turn," said Ted. "You said 'it tops your news', you haven't come all the way to Aberdovey to tell us you've chipped a fingernail. What is it? You're getting married at last?"

Jennifer checked her fingernails. They were, as ever, pristine. A chipped fingernail would ruin her image. "I am, yes!" she declared with a huge grin on her face then flashed a diamond ring on her finger, "to Tony. I'm sailing to America with him next month."

Emma and Ted's mouths were wide open, "Jen! That's fantastic. Oh, I'm so happy for you. About damn time too. What on earth took the pair of you so long?"

Jennifer took out another cigarette and lit up. "After all the years of letter writing backwards and forwards, Tony said it would be cheaper if he came back to convince me to marry him. I told him he was crazy, that it would never work. I'm a Cardiff girl Em, you know that. For goodness sake we were kids when we first met in the First World War. Hmm. I remember the night. Not long after that bombing Em, the one at the Village Hall." Emma shuddered, how could she ever forget that night? and she inwardly prayed Jennifer wouldn't delve any deeper.

"Yeah, it was nice, and then of course all the Yanks went home but we wrote each other - all the time, actually. Then the next war came and once again Tony was in the UK so we arranged to meet up . . . a few times. Can't believe he never married anyone back in the States, he's a good-looking chap, Emma!"

Emma was in no doubt that Tony was a good-looking chap! Her sister, too, was a good-looking woman. She'd never understood why she'd stayed single all her life. Perhaps Tony had always been the real love of her life? Things always happen for a reason.

"Jen, I'm thrilled for you, truly. I'm happy you're going to live in America with this man. Are we going to meet him before you sail? Is this going to be the last time the two of us are going to be together?"

"I'm happy Em, really, but a little afraid too. Gosh I've been single for so many years I don't know how I'm going to fit in over there, all those Yanks!"

Emma and Ted burst out laughing, "they will adore you Jen, how could they possibly not?"

"Mummy Emma, look what I've got!" Billy ran up to her holding a handful of May Blossom, his face beaming, Ivan hovering behind him in the doorway.

Emma took a sharp intake of breath, her hand clutching her neck, and every minute detail of doubt about what she and Ted were doing with these children, evaporated into the ether! Those few words somersaulted in her mind and she instantly felt the most unimaginable emotion that she had never thought possible.

'Mummy Emma . . . ' He'd called her 'Mummy'! She covered her face with her hands as she blubbered like a baby. Billy looked mortified, he hadn't meant to upset her. "I'm sorry, I'm sorry," he repeated.

"Billy, NO, don't be sorry," Emma tried to reassure him, injecting laughter into her reply, "these flowers are just the most beautiful flowers I have ever seen, and they made me want to cry. Thank you so much. Do you know what? I'm going to put them in some water and have them on our table so that when we have breakfast in the morning, we can all see and smell them. And when they're nearly over, I'm going to press them in my diary so that I will remember this day forever."

"And Marley's birthday?"

"And Marley's birthday, too. It's been a very special day today."

Billy stood by Emma's side, he looked across at Jennifer, at Ted and Ivan, and then at Marley who was on the floor putting a burst balloon into her mouth. He turned to Emma, smiling, "you're my best mammy".

18 May 1946 would be Emma's most favourably memorable day. "Out of the mouths of babes..." her heart

burst. She had come to realise that she couldn't have loved her own flesh and blood any more than she had come to love these two foundlings. Her sister had come to visit and they'd made their peace, having barely seen each other since they were teenagers. Like she said earlier, the war was over, there would be no more battles to fight.

Chapter 12: Ivan's New Leg

Ted needed to leave Ivan alone to attend to the flock and all the other animals, claiming he had to go into town to collect supplies. "Billy, I could do with your help this morning in Aberdovey. Will you get dressed and come with me?"

Billy looked horrified! He didn't know what 'town' was. He knew it was a place where Ted and Emma went to go and came back with supplies but he'd never been to one. He'd never been anywhere before, until he came to Trefellon! In fact he couldn't remember seeing another person other than his 'mammy' and the man - Terry.

He'd never seen a swing before, it was a fun thing and he loved to go outside in the sunshine and sit on it and rock. He'd learned to hold on to the ropes, swaying forwards and backwards, and he tilted his head up to the sky and looked at the funny clouds. Sometimes he would see images in the clouds like a leg or a tree. He liked the clouds, they looked soft and fluffy.

He once saw something in the sky which he thought was so pretty. It was lots of different colours in the shape of an arc. He imagined the sky must be a beautiful place to live because the birds he watched, flew and swooped and made lovely trill sounds. But he wasn't outside much at all in those early days, only to go to the lavvy and the lavvy was a horrible place. It hurt his nose and tummy and made him feel sick but if didn't go, and mess himself, the man would be angry and he'd be scolded.

Billy liked his new mammy better than his other one because his other one didn't make nice food, like Emma did, or as often. This 'Mammy Emma' had a happy face and she talked to him and Marley softly. She smelled nice too, and so did he and Marley. He loved the big tin bath that she put in front of the roaring range every Friday night with nice hot water, and he would feel her smooth hands washing his body with a sweet-smelling soap. And then the man 'Mammy Ted' would wrap him up in a big warm towel as he lifted him out of the water and dry him rigorously, all the while chattering away saying things like "Billy, you look like baby Jesus."

He wasn't convinced 'baby Jesus' was a nice thing to say because the 'man' would say "Jesus Christ!" in a bad way: his face would be red and he'd hit his mammy when he said it. But this man's face didn't go red when *he* said it, he smiled when he did.

So - was 'going to town' going to be a good thing, or what? *'I could do with your help'*. Billy decided his help was needed so he ran up the stairs to get himself dressed. Seconds later he was in the truck waiting for Ted.

"Ha, it's alright for some to go gallivanting in town this morning leaving me and Boo to collect all the eggs," said Ivan, leaning one elbow on the wound-down window, the other on his crutch, and then Billy did something he'd never done before . . . he stuck his tongue out to Ivan! Neither was sure as to who was the most surprised, but Ivan roared with laughter and did exactly the same back, both of them laughing at each other.

Billy sat smiling in the grown-up seat next to Ted, all the way to Aberdovey as he watched the picturesque scenery unfolding before him, the magnificent purple rhododendrons in abundance along the roads, Ted pointing out various places of interest and waving to a familiar face en route.

They arrived at the post office. The very same post office where, years before, Ted had bumped into Emma, his now wife. "Billy. You and I are here to collect a surprise for our Ivan." He sniggered, "it's our gift to him, to thank him for all his help and that's why I asked you to come with me this morning." Billy looked at Ted, blankly.

"Ahh. Ivan gives everyone the impression of being blasé. I know you won't understand what blasé means, but it means he *pretends* he doesn't care about his missing leg. Well of course he does, any man would, but I also recognise it's a war wound of which he will be forever proud to bear. It speaks to everyone, lets everyone know that he did his duty."

He turned to look at Billy, who was already looking at him, confused. "Ivan Rhys is a war hero, Billy, he doesn't like to tell folk, doesn't like to draw too much attention to himself." Ted cocked his head towards Billy. "Doesn't sound like the Ivan you know, hey? Haha. Eiffion always loved an audience, sorry, Ivan. Ivan loves an audience, but he's not a braggart. No. I've heard snippets going round this place of his heroism but he's never whispered a word. Mark my words, Billy lad, our dear friend is more than meets the eye. Now then, let's go and get his surprise."

They collected a large package from the post office which Ted placed on the back seat of the truck. He turned the ignition key, "home James, and don't spare the horses," he chuckled to himself, the phrase being totally lost on Billy who was looking bewildered as he could see no horses.

"Years ago, Billy, way before you were born, everybody had horses and carriages as their transport. No motor vehicles had been invented then, and that was the expression used, to hurry them along, *'Don't spare the horses.'*" Ted pondered his words, "cruel really, Billy. Totally unnecessary."

They arrived back at Trefellon and Ted lifted Billy out of the truck. Ivan was sat outside with Emma, Marley and Boo and Billy ran over to join them. "Ivan, Ivan, quickly. Come and see, Mammy Ted has a surprise for ye."

Exchanged glances, raised eyebrows and smiles all round. Ivan would definitely store that into his memory bank. 'Mammy Ted'? He would have so much fun!

Ted walked over to join them as they sat outside on the grassy area, holding a large package in his hands. Billy stood there smiling and gazing at Ted as he held out the package to Ivan. Ivan held out his hands to receive the package, looking around for confirmation from Emma, who just shrugged, smiling.

"Ivan, I want you to know how much we all appreciate you. All of us, don't we Billy?" he said, looking straight at him, "and . . . well, we want to give you this, so you'll be able to work a bit faster, but if this means you're gonna run away from us, then I'll burn the bloody thing I swear."

All eyes watched as Ivan unwrapped the package. He held up a prosthetic leg high in the air and laughed and laughed. He threw down his crutch as he sat on a stone boulder, attempting to fasten it on to his thigh. He'd seen them before, crude metal frames which resembled a leg not a jot! He'd vowed never to have one, but this one was different, it actually 'looked' like a *real* leg.

Giggling like a schoolboy, Ivan and Emma tried to fix it to his stump, and it fit! It felt comfortable too, and Ivan stood up, tottering about on two legs for the first time since he felt that excruciating pain in his kneecap which felled him to the ground. He recalled placing his hand there, feeling the warm blood gushing over him and he thought he was going to die, right there and then.

He picked up his crutch, placing it under his armpit as he tried out his new leg, walking a few intrepid steps, constantly watching the reactions of his audience. He sat back down on the boulder and roared with laughter, "it itches," he said out loud, "my big toe, it itches!"

Everybody was laughing with him, except Billy who no longer was laughing. "Is this just until your leg grows back Ivan?", he asked, sincerely.

"No, Billy. My leg will never grow back. Did you think it would?"

"My hair grows back, and Marley's bottom growed back. The sheep's wool grows back and Boo's nails when they've been clipped. Why won't your leg grow back?"

What a question, Ivan thought to himself, and how to explain that to a four-year-old. "Billy, you are such a clever boy. Yes, indeed your hair will grow again after it's been cut, and your fingernails, and Marley's bottom was healed because Emma put some healing creams on her. Not magic, just healing herbs. A human-being can't regrow a missing limb, Billy. Not like certain reptiles, they can."

'A reptile', Billy pondered. Another word he'd never heard before.

The **excitement** of the occasion shifted as all eyes surveyed Ivan who seemed to have lost himself in his thoughts.

This gift! This selfless gift that Ted and Emma had spent **their** hard-earned money on, touched him deeply and he wanted to turn away from their hopeful expressions whilst he reflected on his feelings when he first realised the finality and obstacles he was coming to have to confront when the war – *if* the war – eventually came to conclusion, returning home a 'cripple', but he couldn't. He had a watchful audience.

He recalled the words he'd heard the pretty young nurse tell him that they'd had to remove part of his lower leg. 'How could *that* be?' he asked himself, he'd only suffered a minor injury. His hand reached underneath the bedclothes in disbelief and tried in vain to stifle a sob as his fingers touched the bandages, the confirmation of her words hurting his ears.

He saw his future crash and burn in front of him. He immediately worried that Davy would skedaddle and find a more able-bodied 'friend' with whom he could continue to dance the nights away.

And then he thought of James. James, and the millions of other young men like him who didn't have the second chance he'd been given - and was ashamed.

Ivan rose, balancing from one leg to his 'other' leg. He tentatively took steps putting one in front of the other, laughing all the time. "Mrs T," he said dramatically, "I'm in LOVE with your husband!"

"If you can force your heart and nerve and sinew

To serve your turn long after they are gone,

And so hold on when there is nothing in you

Except the Will which says to them: 'Hold on'"

Rudyard Kipling

Chapter 13: Two Years Later

Emma had blinked and Marley had become a walking nightmare! She was into everything, having learned how to open cupboard doors, emptying the contents all over the kitchen floor at every opportunity. She would eat Boo's food from her bowl, she would pick up pieces of coal from the coal skuttle and suck them, her mouth and clothing constantly black. Billy, on the other hand, was a comparative angel and rarely needed telling off. It was hard to decipher their sexes sometimes, Marley most definitely a 'tom-boy'. She'd protest at wearing dresses, throwing tantrums until she was allowed to wear trousers, like her brother did to school.

None of the locals questioned their being at Trefellon any longer, assuming the Talberts were now their legal guardians, but Emma and Ted knew they had to do something in the not-too-distant future to ensure they couldn't be taken away as flippantly as they had been dumped in their barn. They wanted everything above-board and legal and were adamant they would put up a fight if the situation arose.

Billy had been going to school now for almost two years and he loved it. He made a friend on his first day who became a best friend; he called her 'Zero' - her real name was Sarah. When he arrived home after his first nerve-racking day out of the comfort of Trefellon, he was bubbling over with excitement. It had been so easy getting him in at school, Emma had been relieved that the process wasn't as daunting as she and Ted had anticipated. Both had pre-visited the school to ascertain the fundamentals of him starting. When asked his name and date-of-birth Emma replied 'Billy Talbert, 3rd November 1942' and a week later she was back at the school standing in Miss Bevan's class with about twenty children – all approximately Billy's age - with Billy crying and begging her not to leave him. It quite tore at her heart strings to see him so agitated and upset, reassuring him that he was going to have fun with Miss Bevan and all the other children. Miss Bevan took Billy's hand and sat him next to a little girl with blonde pigtails.

"Class, we have a new boy with us today and his name is Billy Talbert. What do we say when we have someone new join us?" announced Miss Bevan to her class.

"Welcome Billy Talbert," they all droned. Billy was confused, he didn't know he had two names.

"I'm Sarah," said the little blonde pigtailed girl sitting next to him. (Zero? what a funny name, thought Billy.)

Ted and Ivan were shearing the sheep one day when Ted began to discuss their options with the children. Ivan always seemed to have a wealth of knowledge about practically everything. "Emma and I want to make the children legally ours, Ivan. We couldn't bear to lose them after all this time."

Ivan nodded. Neither would he. He'd formed a really tight bond with Billy and he saw a lot of his previous self in him. Billy was sensitive, he was kind to the animals and sobbed bitterly when the butcher appeared at the farm. He refused to eat meat anymore, announcing that he would not eat 'babies'. The animals were his friends and so was Boo. He wouldn't eat Boo and he wouldn't eat Grannie Annie. (*Grannie Annie was formerly Annie, but Annie's baby rabbits very soon had babies of their own.*) No, he

99

announced one Sunday dinnertime with tears streaming down his face, please don't make me eat them.

Emma was at her wits end, worrying constantly about his eating habits, but Billy was content to eat anything and everything other than his 'friends'.

One insignificant, warm and sunny Sunday afternoon that August, Emma sat outside on a boulder next to the water pump, washing the carrots, beetroot and cauliflower in preparation for Ted to take to Aberdovey to sell. The cottage windows had been opened to allow the summer sun inside, the wireless was playing and Emma was singing along to "I'm looking over a four leaf clover", a song she resonated with as she used to find them in their meadows, scores of them. She still had the very first one she ever found! She recalled that moment of excitement, not at first sure it *did* have four leaves until she picked it. "Ted," she squealed, "we're gonna be lucky."

It became an obsession of hers, looking for and finding so many. She must have picked a few hundred over the years, pressing them into books and once they'd dried out sufficiently, she'd put one inside a birthday card or Christmas card and post them to family and friends.

The wireless continued to play as Emma and Billy sat listening. Suddenly, Sammy Kaye's 'Lavender Blue' was pealing out. Emma almost choked with laughing as Billy rose up and started to dance. He was singing along to the song, (*obviously heard it before*) and then she stopped what she was doing and watched him, mesmerized.

"Lavender blue, dilly, dilly, lavender green . . . ", he was twirling, leaping and bowing, his face was a picture of joy and Emma watched as her 'little boy' gracefully danced in front of her. She watched as his arms swayed rhythmically in time with the music, his foot pointed against his calf as he attempted a pirouette, which he succeeded in doing. Emma's mouth was wide open in amusement so she threw down the vegetables she was cleaning and joined him. She took his hands and danced with him. "When you are King, Billy, Billy, I'll be your queen."

As they finished dancing and laughing, Emma looked over at Billy, acknowledging something she'd never noticed before. He resembled Ivan in *so* many ways. Not in looks, no it wasn't that; they bore no physical likeness whatsoever, but there was *something*... Their demeanour and mannerisms, their idiosyncrasies. Was it nurture, or was it nature? Was he mimicking his hero or was he growing into *himself*? He was most definitely the easier of the two children of that there was no doubt. Billy was at his happiest when he was helping out around the farm and he thrived on the praise he received. He inwardly shrank if he accidently broke an egg he'd collected from the chicken coop, apologising over and over.

Billy had never uttered a word about his past. Emma had cautiously pushed for a couple of answers but garnered nothing. It was almost as if the boy had been locked away, out of sight, for he knew nothing about anything. She assumed he must have had a dog because he took to Boo, calling her 'Bonny Lass', and he had never been afraid of her.

He'd stopped asking for his mammy, too, though Emma was sure he must still remember her. What kind of life had he known? He never talked about having toys, friends, family, and if he had had a dog, he never even talked about that!

One night when she went into the little bedroom to check on them, she found Billy sitting atop the ottoman, underneath the window, staring up into the night sky. "If I gave you a penny for every star you count Billy, how many pennies would I have to give you?"

He turned to look at Emma, "what's a star?" he asked. She looked up out of the window, "all those bright shiny lights in the sky, they're called stars. They're always there even though sometimes we can't see them." She put her arm around him, "they're beautiful aren't they?" Billy nodded.

Ted and Ivan walked into the kitchen having had a very trying day, Ivan no longer needing the support of his crutch. They'd been late with the sheep shearing this year due to essential roofing repairs needed on the barn and the sheep pen. Water had poured in, saturating the feed and the bedding.

"Smells divine in here, Mrs T. What culinary delights have you cooked tonight?" asked Ivan.

"Aubergine and cauliflower bake, and Billy helped to chop the tomatoes. Ted, move Boo's bowl from there, put it on top of the work-surface, Marley's already eaten half of it!"

"I'm going to Aberdovey in the morning, Em, to see that solicitor chap. We've been talking about it today, me and

Ivan. You and I have discussed it many times and it's about time we got things settled."

Emma placed a bowl of mashed potatoes on the table, "Marley! Come and sit up – now!" then smiled at everyone, "help yourselves."

"Aubergine and Cauliflower bake, hmm. I must say, Mrs T, I never imagined a dinner without meat. My dear old grandma used to keep pigs and she always said 'the only thing you couldn't eat of a pig was its squeal'" Billy gasped, "but I must say, I am quite enjoying this vegetarian thingy, it's real tasty! And, err .. is that Gooseberry crumble for pudding I can smell over there?"

Chapter 14: Legalities

August Mensah had moved to Aberdovey to try to re-establish himself in the world of legalities. He was a sorry drunkard, discredited from his previous post in a small law firm in Birmingham.

Ted never paid heed to gossip; he didn't know what the man's past had been so he would neither judge nor cast aspersions. If it was true that he was a drunkard it could be possible that he had been at war and who knew what horrors and demons the man had had to contend with? All *they* needed a man of the law for was to make them the children's legal guardians, by adoption if that was going to be possible! It wasn't as if they needed a defence lawyer!

Emma, Ted and Ivan had talked for hours about the possible procedure and what stumbling blocks and barriers they could expect to encounter. If all went according to their plans, they could soon legally be parents and nobody could come back and make a claim on them.

Sat inside August Mensah's humble office Ted began to talk. He told him how the children had come to be in their care. How they'd parented them, nurtured them, *love* them.

"And you have no idea who these children belong to, where they came from?" August asked.

Emma and Ted looked at each other, hadn't they just told him that?

"No," said Ted, a little sharper than Emma worried he should have done. "My farm hand thinks they may have come from somewhere in Scotland as the boy had an accent that was most definitely not from around these parts. They were not in the best of health I might add. Very pasty, almost as if they'd been kept inside all the time. They've been with us for well over two years now, coming up to three, and they've improved ten-fold. The lad is at school and loves it, he's got friends there. He's never spoken a word about his past. He regards us, my wife and I and our farm hand, as his family. The girl has only ever known us."

"Mmm, mmm, yes I understand. Difficult this. Never heard of anything like this before."

August Mensah was quite a pitiful-looking man. He was painfully thin and his hands trembled. On his left hand he had two missing fingers, his pinkie and his wedding finger. If he was married it wasn't evident because he wouldn't have been able to wear a wedding band. His dark-grey suit buried him and his shirt collar was dingy and fraying. Emma thought that if he did have a wife she would have turned his collar, that's what wives did. She felt sorry for him.

"I want our children to be able to call us Mummy and Daddy, because that's what they are – our children."

"Yes, yes, I understand. Well, leave it with me. I'll get on to this. Very odd situation, but I feel quite optimistic." August ran his right hand through his thinning, dark hair. He must have only been in his forties, yet he looked much older.

"Your farm hand, does he have much interaction with these children? Can we count on him as a character witness, to vouch for you?" he asked.

"Ivan loves the kiddies as much as we do. He's been a Godsend. Yes, indeed you can," replied Ted.

Emma and Ted left the office, not altogether confident but feeling somewhat hopeful.

They'd told Billy that they would collect him from school and that he was to wait there until they arrived. Usually, he would walk – there and back, a long journey but he met up with several other children en route, 'Zero' included. They pulled up at the school entrance expecting to find Billy and when Miss Bevan saw them she hurried towards them, her huge frame wobbling as she made haste.

"Oh dear me, Mrs Talbert, I'm so sorry but Billy's at the hospital, he's been very poorly, sick as a dog he's been, and then he collapsed. He told me you would be collecting him from school today, so I waited to tell you . . "

Ted didn't wait to listen the rest of what Miss Bevan was saying as he swung the truck into reverse and drove straight to the hospital.

Billy was lying on a metal-framed hospital bed, his deep red hair wet with perspiration, his freckled nose beaded with sweat, a young nurse at his bedside checking his pulse. He was awake but appeared confused. He spotted Ted and Emma and burst into tears, reaching out to them, "Mummy Emma am I going to die after it?" he cried.

Emma glared at Ted, remembering his words when he fell off the swing all that time ago, seemingly the child had not forgotten. She rushed to take his hand, "it's okay sweetheart, we're here, you're going to be just fine," she hoped!

"Well, I think this young man can go home once the doctor gives his say-so. We did think he may have had meningitis, in fact his teacher suggested that when someone from the school brought him in but it doesn't appear that way. He has been sick and a slight temperature but nothing that definitely points to meningitis," the young nurse confirmed, "perhaps a touch of food poisoning?"

Emma was livid! "Food poisoning! He doesn't eat any meat and if it was food poisoning why haven't the rest of our family been sick?"

Ted was trying to calm her down but she was boiling! Whatever had caused Billy to end up in the hospital was nothing she had done! She couldn't wait for the doctor to come round and tell them he was fit to leave and return home.

They sat in the truck, driving back to the farm, Billy in between the two of them, Emma's arm around his shoulders. "I'm sorry," Billy said, turning to Emma. "Don't be, it's not your fault. Sometimes people get sick and that's why we have doctors to make us better again. How are you feeling now?"

"Hungry," he replied.

Whatever had caused Billy to end up in the hospital remained a mystery. He returned to school the next morning as right as rain and bright as a button. He couldn't wait to meet up with 'Zero' and his other friends and tell them all about his exciting adventure. He felt quite important, none of his friends had ever been in a hospital! The minor trauma had given him leverage with his classmates, making him almost heroic!

Five more long anxious months passed with no word from August Mensah. Ivan had, on numerous occasions, hinted that Ted should call in to nudge him, ask for an update on proceedings. "Mr T, these children will be forever foundlings if you don't sign some papers pretty soon."

Ted, Ivan and Emma sat in the kitchen having an elevenses and a slice of homemade fruit cake when there was a knock at the door. It was August, looking perpetually the dishevelled, waif-like man they'd seen before. "I come bearing good news!"

"Mr Mensah! How lovely of you to call. Tea, and a slice of cake?"

He looked around at the table and almost stumbled onto a chair. "I'm so sorry to have taken so long, difficult situation this, complicated. Thank you, yes, no sugar."

Ivan stifled a snigger.

"I contacted a fellow I knew; we were in the war together. His father dealt with many similar cases years ago. Children from the workhouses. He managed to reunite some with their families and others he managed to secure adoption to childless couples, so I talked with him – about your children - and he arranged for me to meet his father. Excellent chap, he is, too. Yes, very knowledgeable, he helped me no end."

Everyone sat up straight, eager to listen to more. "I've got the adoption papers here, now all I need is your signatures. These will then be sent off to the authorities. Oh, I don't need to bother you with all the inconsequentialities, and once my fee has been paid, I will present the adoptive birth certificates to you."

"So... once we sign these documents, the children are now legally ours?" asked Ted, not quite being able to believe it.

"As soon as you sign on the dotted line."

Emma moved from her seat and went over to the pathetic man who had just bestowed the most amazing gift to her and hugged him. "Thank you. Thank you so much Mr Mensah - sir."

He giggled.

"Please let me give you a little thank-you gift," Emma said, moving away and taking a bottle of Sloe Gin from the kitchen cupboard, "enjoy," she said, smiling.

"Mr Mensah, we're going to have bit of a family celebration this weekend and we insist you join us for dinner and drinks. Next Saturday, six pm? I can collect and return you so that you can have a drink without the worry of driving back."

August Mensah looked at Ted, then at Emma and Ivan's anticipated smiling faces. He tried to remember the last time he'd received such an invitation, he almost wept as he stuttered an affirmative, and left.

As he stood at his car and opened the door, Mensah turned to the sounds of squeals and laugher bellowing from the warm hospitality of the cottage and tried to imagine the scene, their excitement, whilst acknowledging how lucky those two children were to have ended up here in Aberdovey with these people who obviously cared for them so much. It was a far cry from the life August Mensah had endured under the iron rod of his own brutal, alcoholic mother.

Mensah had been glad to receive his call-up papers, back then, to escape her apron-strings, do his bit, and be able to integrate with real men. How lucky these children were, to be spared the life he had. Not that anyone did have any background information, but he wished he had been repositioned into a family where he was welcomed, loved, and wanted.

He sat for a moment in his car and reached into the glove compartment for his hip flask that contained brandy, contemplating whether to open the gifted bottle of sloe gin or to take yet another swig from his flask. He hated himself for being this way, but what better example had he other than that of his own mother? His father had been killed during the First World War, shot in front of a firing squad for desertion.

August Mensah never knew the full details, only the snippets he heard from the whispers in the inns his mother frequented nightly. Birmingham had many such establishments full of drunken soldiers on leave, willing to part with some of their cash for a bit of female comfort before returning to the depths of their despair.

Chapter 15: Billy and Ivan

Billy ran up to his bedroom after his friends had left his birthday party. He'd invited his whole class and only four had turned up, 'Zero' plus three others, all girls. He was embarrassed that his mother had laid a table full of sandwiches, sausage rolls, desserts, cake, all the food that parties have. He was disappointed that the girls had turned up and not the boys, he was nine years old and that fact was wounding. He was going to suffer at school the next day, that was for certain. He was going to be teased and tormented - again.

He could never understand what he was doing wrong or why the other boys didn't ask him to join them at play times. 'Zero' (Sarah) was the only one who really talked with him. "They're all jealous of you Billy, that's why they don't ask you."

"Jealous? Of me? But why?" he asked.

She studied him, "duh! Because you're clever and they're stupid. Because you live on a farm and they don't, they live in tiny houses you have the great big farm that supplies the whole of our village with food. Their fathers are miners, those that still have them; some of the dads didn't come back from the war, remember. And you are adopted, that means you're special; your parents wanted you and Marley, it's not like that for the rest of us." Billy contemplated her answer. He hadn't thought about it that way.

"Not only that Billy-boy, but *you* are special, you're different to that lot. My mum says you have potential and that one day your name will be up in lights."

"What's potential?" he asked.

"How do I know? But whatever it is, you have it."

Ivan walked up the stairs after Billy, gently tapping on his door "Billy, would you care to join me in the barn, I have something I'd like to show you."

Billy didn't really want to leave his bedroom, he just wanted to curl up under the security of his eiderdown and hide, but Ivan wasn't going to be deterred and perched himself on the edge of his bed. "When I was your age, at school, I didn't have any friends."

Billy poked his head out; he'd never ignore Ivan.

116

"At least you have Sarah, and she's a good friend an' all. I was bullied, and I think you're being bullied, too. I'm not going to let you answer until you hear what I have to say.

I had a pretty rough time growing up here in Aberdovey. See; my father was a miner and I wasn't the kind of son he wanted. He'd always assumed I'd follow in his footsteps and go down the mine but that wasn't at all what I wanted. Me, Billy, I wanted to entertain! I wanted to dance, to act, to be on stage and perform to a waiting audience. I wanted to hear the music and sing at the top of my voice and feel it pulsating through me. I *needed* to express myself through dance and song. You know, the happiest time of my life was when I was at war."

Billy looked aghast at Ivan not comprehending how anyone's happiest times could have been at war. The fighting, the bloodshed, never knowing if you would be alive in the next minute or not.

"It gave me the opportunity to mix with like-minded people, men like me, and oh there were so many of us, all colluding under the umbrella of bravado. We were scared shitless Billy, pardon my French, everybody was but it made our odyssey not... bearable, no that's not the word

117

I'm looking for... I suppose what I'm trying to get across is that when you're with people who understand you and want the same as you, it makes life's journey more worthwhile. More bearable.

I went to Scotland, you know, before the war broke out. I was living my dream in Edinburgh, fabulous city. I was there, entertaining people who were paying to watch me dance and sing and act. I'm thinking of returning soon, I have good friends waiting for me. Coming back to Aberdovey when the war finished was only meant to be a fleeting visit, but then I met your dear dad and the rest you know."

"You're going to leave?" Billy asked.

"This 'fleeting visit' has lasted over six years sweet boy, I may not be able to trip the light fantastic anymore or manage a pas-de-deux," he joked, tapping his prosthetic leg, "but the old vocal cords and charisma are still in abundance and I'm sure I can be able to thrill an audience or two."

Billy felt strange. He couldn't imagine his life at Trefellon without Ivan, he'd always been around; the constant joker, fixer of everything, a walking encyclopaedia, a best friend and father-figure. His mentor!

"So worry ye not about the lack of male testosterone at your birthday party today, young man, 'tis they who have missed out, not us. Now then, will you come with me to the barn to see what I have for you?"

Ivan had a record player - all set up. Billy had never seen anything like it, it looked so modern, so complicated! The floor had been cleared of debris so that the earth was showing, a lamp hung overhead, casting a down-shadow. Ivan quickly turned the handle on the record player and the music started, a familiar song that Billy had heard many times before and he smiled at Ivan.

"Dance then, Billy lad. Come on, I want to see how the music makes you feel."

Billy looked at him, confused.

"I've seen you dance and I've heard you sing. You know this song, now go for it!"

And Billy danced, and he sang, "Lavender blue, dilly, dilly..." his freckled face laughed as he twirled, jumped, spun. His arms in the air then gracefully forming an almost perfect 'port de bras'.

Ivan watched in amazement. The boy had talent and no one was the slightest bit aware! He put another record on the deck, one he knew Billy hadn't heard before, "a different one for you now. Dance it and feel it and tell me how it makes you feel." It was one of Tchaikovsky's Swan Lake compositions: a favourite of Ivan's.

Billy stood listening for a few minutes as the record played, watching Ivan all the time. His smile turned to sadness. "It makes me feel sad, but it also makes me want to fly. It makes me not bothered about anything or anyone," he said.

"Then fly, Billy, fly!" And as he watched Billy feel the music, he knew he'd made the right decision.

Emma was standing in the doorway shouting for Boo to come inside. She was an old dog now and even though her hearing was on the decline, her speed and agility were the same as if she was still a puppy dog - in that way - no one would ever believe she was thirteen years old.

She heard the music coming from the barn and it was beautiful music that drew her towards it. She stood outside for a second or two, not wishing to eavesdrop but nevertheless intrigued.

She was surprised to hear Billy's laughter and Ivan's, relieved to presume Billy had forgotten his earlier dismay at the lack of his friends at his party. She knocked at the barn door and walked in.

"Ah, Mrs T, do come in," Ivan said jovially, "your boy here is just receiving my birthday gift to him. Go on then, Billy, I'll put the record on again."

He looked apprehensive at first, then once the music was playing, he danced. He danced until the music stopped and Emma clapped and clapped, "that was the most beautiful thing I have ever seen, Billy, you were wonderful, but it's past your bedtime now, time to come inside."

As she walked back inside the cottage with Billy a thought appeared to her, it wasn't nurture - it *was* nature. Billy was *exactly* like Ivan. How could she have missed something that she now realised was so obvious? It was as though she had just woken up. Had Ivan come to the same conclusion, or had it not even crossed his mind? Maybe it had; perhaps he had seen his younger self in Billy and that was why the two got on so well.

Emma felt a slight apprehension as she thought back to the persecution Ivan had suffered growing up, worried that Billy would undoubtedly endure the same taunts, ridicule, bullying. She would hate that, knowing that children can be so very cruel.

Chapter 16: Confrontation

"I'm hoping to leave Wales at the end of the month Mr T; coming back to Aberdovey was only supposed to be a fleeting visit but it's been many years, you understand?"

Ted was taken aback! Yes, he knew Ivan hadn't planned on staying so long but he never wanted to acknowledge that he'd eventually up sticks and leave them all. He knew he loved the children, especially Billy, just as much as he and Emma, but even so, he was saddened to hear his news - even more so with his next bombshell!

". . and I want to take Billy with me."

Ted stopped with his hammering, looking seriously at Ivan, then burst out laughing, assuming he was joking.

"I want to take the boy out of this place and make him somebody. I can't bear the thought of Billy enduring the same traumas I did, here."

"Ivan! He's a child," he laughed, "he's still at school. He's got his whole life ahead of him . . ."

"And what life, Ted?" he interrupted, no longer using his previous familiar 'Mr T' address, "being bullied and persecuted, ridiculed because of the way he is? Like I was?"

Ted glared at him in disbelief. "The boy lives here, with us," he said sternly, "we adopted him, both of them. You want to take Marley too? Are we not good enough to be their parents, is that what you're insinuating? By God, Ivan, what on earth has got into your head? Of course you can't bloody well take him and make him - what? Somebody? He already *is* 'somebody', he's our son, or have you forgotten?"

Ivan wasn't finished. "You gave me a fresh start here, a chance that folk round these parts weren't too willing to do and I'm forever indebted to you both. Likewise, I want to repay you by giving Billy the same kind of chances that you gave me. A life - because you can bet your bottom dollar it won't happen here, Ted. He's already being bullied every day at school, or have you not noticed? The longer he stays here in Aberdovey the quicker he will inwardly die."

Ted was furious. He stormed off, eager to get away from Ivan. He'd heard enough – too much. How dare he? After all they'd done for him and this is how he wants to repay them, by taking away his pride and joy. The nerve of the man!

"Go," he yelled, "don't bother waiting till the end of the month just pack your bloody stuff up and bugger off."

Which was exactly the reaction Ivan had anticipated.

Ted was spitting feathers; he could not imagine what had possessed the man to come out with such an inane suggestion. The boy is not something to be passed about from pillar to post. He needed stability and he and Emma had given both the children just that. Yes, he knew all about Ivan's persecution growing up, it hadn't been easy for him and everyone knew the reasons he left to start a new life in Scotland.

He recalled one time he was coming back from the market and saw a group of lads involved in a kerfuffle, Ivan was on the floor being punched and kicked. As Ted shouted, running over to intervene, the boys scarpered, and Ivan wiped his bloodied nose at the back of his hand, laughing. "Thank you, Mr Talbert," he said, "don't worry, no real harm done; it's all character building," and up he jumped and strode away.

But Billy wasn't Ivan, he was not as strong, either mentally *or* physically. He was sensitive, and a situation like that would be devastating for him.

Was he being selfish? Was he simply denying his son a different kind of life to the one he'd earmarked for him? He was hoping to hand over Trefellon to him when the time came to pass and he and Emma could retire to a smaller cottage somewhere. There would be grandchildren to enjoy, a whole new generation of Talberts. What did he mean 'he would inwardly die'? What hadn't *he* noticed that Ivan did? Or more to the point, what was he not acknowledging?

He was confused yet still angry. He knew that Emma would share his vexation so there would be no chance of a discussion. The subject was closed: he would need to find a new farm hand.

The four began to congregate at the table for their evening meal. "Where's Ivan?" Emma asked nonchalantly passing plates to everyone, his seat remaining unoccupied.

"He won't be joining us."

"Why not?"

"He has decided it's time to leave Wales. He'll not be joining us again."

"What?" cried Emma.

"What?" whispered Billy.

Marley sat looking from Ted to Emma, then picked up her knife and fork. Nothing upset her appetite!

"Where is he now?" asked Billy.

"He went to collect his belongings. Perhaps he's left already."

Billy leapt from the table and ran outside to find him, hoping he wasn't too late . . . but he was! The barn was silent and all that was left of Ivan was the record player, a hand-written note propped against it, '*Billy, feel the music, keep dancing. Ivan.*'

He was distraught and ran back inside the house, sobbing "he's gone, he's gone and didn't even say goodbye. Dad, what did you do to make him go away? I don't want him to leave. Please, make him come back home."

Emma didn't know what was happening. It was so unlike Ivan. Indeed, what *had* Ted done or said to make him leave so quickly, and without saying goodbye to them all? It didn't make any sense.

"He wanted to go back to Edinburgh to fulfil his dreams, I suppose," Ted shrugged.

"How will we manage without him? Ted, what are we going to do?"

"Dammit Em, I don't know, he only told me this afternoon. I'll go into town tomorrow and find someone else, I'm sure there are lots of people there who would be only too happy for some work. We both knew Ivan wasn't going to stay here forever, for God's sake!" His retort quite shocked her and she realised there must have been more to their conversation than Ted was letting on.

Billy was still sobbing. He didn't want any dinner and he did not want to be pacified. Ivan had been his mentor, the person he sought out the most when he needed a friend; the one who seemed to understand him more than his parents or Sarah, and the only person he completely aspired to. He felt an overwhelming feeling of hatred towards his dad and stormed upstairs to his bedroom refusing to talk to anyone.

Ivan sat at the train station waiting for the nine thirty train to take him to Birmingham; from there he would have to wait until the following morning for the first train to Edinburgh. He was feeling despondent, hating to leave under such a gloomy cloud, never having the opportunity to thank Emma for everything she'd done for him, and not being able to explain to Billy the reasons for his hasty departure.

He hadn't many possessions – didn't need them. He had money, he'd saved all his wages, never having the necessity to spend it, apart from buying the odd pair of boots or clothing.

He'd written to his old war pal, Hank Ralston, a few weeks beforehand, asking if he could source some suitable accommodation.   Nothing fancy and certainly nothing expensive. He wrote of his plans to return to Edinburgh and eventually open a bar, somewhere big enough to stage events such as cabarets, talent shows, singers, dancers, musicians, etc. He wanted to teach, too. He'd love to be able to reach out to young people and encourage them to dance and act.   He hadn't any qualifications for doing such but he knew how it should all be done and he felt he had the capability, enthusiasm, and wherewithal.   He collected Hank's reply from the post office and was overjoyed with his response!

As he sat eating an apple and reading the timetable on the train station wall, he saw an all too familiar figure frantically searching the platform, and practically choked on his apple.

Chapter 17: Leaving

"Billy! Billy, what in God's name are you doing here, lad?"

Billy fell into his embrace, exhausted. "Why are you going? You didn't tell me! I tell you everything and then you just decide to go without a word?"

The station master blew his whistle, a shrill, piercing sound announcing the arrival of the train to Birmingham, the billowing sulphur-stinking steam from the train's chimney getting closer and closer. 'Next train to Birmingham - platform two.'

Ivan was frantic. He couldn't not board this train! He'd made his plans and all the wheels of his future were set in motion. "Billy, lad. Billy - your folks will be going mental. You're supposed to be in bed, it's way past your bed-time!"

"I want to be with you. I'm not going back." He was crying, trying to catch his breath and Ivan had to quickly consider his options. He could either forget his train and take Billy home, knowing how he feared being in the dark, or he could take him with him and send Ted and Emma a telegram when they arrived in Birmingham though he doubted Ted would believe his story for a second.

Decision made, he grabbed Billy's hand and they boarded the train; Ivan smiled to himself but with anticipation. He knew that his previous friend and employer would be furious but consoled himself knowing that he would be spared the unpleasant task of actually facing him.

They found an empty carriage and went inside, Billy taking his seat next to the window, an apprehensive expression replacing his tears. "Where are we going?" he asked. "To your birthplace, Billy. Scotland: Edinburgh, to be precise. I have special friends there."

Billy raised his eyebrows. Scotland was just a word, to him. He'd never been able to picture it even though he was told that that was where he and Marley might have originally come from. He knew it was a place far away and that he had another mum and dad somewhere, but he could not remember a thing about it, and if he did try to recall anything, it left him feeling unsettled.

They arrived in Birmingham late at night and even though it was night-time Ivan was shocked to see how badly the city had suffered during the Blitz, years ago. He could only imagine the casualties and the suffering.

They were going to spend the next few hours overnight on the station platform, hoping to get a little sleep and in the morning, he would try to find a post office so that he could send the dreaded telegram to Ted.

It was Ivan who awakened first, always being a light sleeper. The slightest whisper in the air, a car backfiring, thunderclaps unnerved him and sent him into a panic. The war would never be over for those who fought at the front. When he closed his eyes to force himself to sleep, he would see his beloved comrades' faces, twisted in agony and bewilderment. The nauseating smell of death constantly tormented his nostrils, he smelt it every single day. His leg still pained him even though it was no longer there. No; every single man that survived that war was still out there, on those battlefields, fighting their own demons, haunting them daily – and nightly. World War Two was from 1939 to 1945? What nonsense!

"Bill," he whispered, nudging the sleeping boy, "Billy, wake up. We have to go and find a post office. We'll look for a café too and get some breakfast; we have just over an hour before our next train leaves."

Billy stirred and looked around him, then quickly jumped up, "are we in Scotland now?" he asked. Ivan laughed out loud, "we're still in Birmingham, got a long way to go yet. Come on."

The post office had only two other customers in the queue, a familiar thin man in a dark suit with a fraying shirt collar stood in front of Ivan and Billy. "Mr Mensah?" enquired Ivan, peering before him.

August Mensah was evidently startled to be recognised, "oh, er, Mr Rhys, my, what a surprise. Ah, and young Billy, hello young man, what a surprise to see you as well." His demeanour confused Ivan, "you in Birmingham on business, Mr Mensah?"

"I am, yes. Yes, I am. Oh dear, is that the time? I can't stop or I'll be late. Look; it's very nice to see you both again. Yes, indeed it is. Do pass on my best wishes to erm, Mr and Mrs Talbert? Yes, thank you. Goodbye, goodbye." And off he scuttled like a rat up a drainpipe!

Ivan and Billy looked at each other and tittered as August Mensah walked out of the post office. Ivan pondered the reasons for the man coming back to Birmingham, having heard the derogatory rumours about his downfall in the practice. Surely he wasn't still welcome here?

The telegram was sent, breakfast consisted of a couple of small loaves from the baker and several slices of ham from the butcher for Ivan and a quarter pound of cheese for Billy, with enough left over for the impending train journey.

When they arrived back at the train station, who should they bump into yet again other than the very same pathetic August Mensah, who literally spat out his tea, all over his newspaper and the table, when he spotted the two people he'd tried very hard earlier to avoid! August quickly rose from his chair, apologising over and over, his words sounding like gobbledegook!

"Mr Mensah, sir, have we done something to upset you? You seem very on edge."

August Mensah hung his head, never meeting Ivan's eyes.

"Whatever it is, it doesn't matter. We have a train to catch. Goodbye sir," Ivan said, turning to Billy to ensure he was ready to make way to their platform.

"But, but that train is going to Edinburgh," August stuttered.

"I know," Ivan answered, "that's where we're going. Oh, and if you see Mr and Mrs Talbert, please let them know that you saw us and that Billy is fine. And let them know that it wasn't my doing. I don't want them to think I kidnapped their son."

"The boy is going with you - to Edinburgh!"

"His choice, though if the law had allowed a single man like me to adopt the boy, then it would have been *my* choice."

They walked away, Ivan and Billy, making their way to the train that had just pulled up.

"But that's just it!" yelled Mensah, running after them, "oh dear, of course I should have done things properly, dotted the i's and crossed the t's and made sure everything was right . . . oh dear, oh dear, I'm so sorry."

Ivan stopped still, turning to look at August, "what do mean, you're sorry?"

"ALL ABOARD FOR EDINBURGH!" echoed down the platform.

Ivan nodded for Billy to mount the steps, climbing behind him holding on to the carriage door handle.

"I'm so sorry, I thought you knew, I thought they were legal, truly!"

"What? You mean to say after all the money they paid you, the adoption isn't legal? Is that what you're sorry about?"

The train began to gather momentum, "I'm sorry, please, it wasn't my fault . . . "

Ivan and Billy sat down gathering their thoughts with neither of them daring to confront what they'd just heard. Billy may only be nine years old but he wasn't deaf and he certainly wasn't stupid. "He didn't do it did he?" he asked, looking at Ivan. "That Mr Mensah, he didn't make us adopted, did he?"

137

Ivan turned to him, took his hands in his, "Billy. In this world there are good, honest folk like your mum and dad and there are people like that vile, lying crook, Mensah. That's the bottom line. You will meet them on every single street corner, wherever you go. You will encounter people who will watch your back and those all too keen to stab you in it. Unfortunately, lad, nobody shouts 'stinking fish' and thankfully there are more good people that walk this earth, than bad. Remember that." Billy had never heard anyone shout 'stinking fish'!

"I've met them all, yes I have." He smiled as he continued, "you want to know the reason I left in a hurry?"

Billy nodded, his expression blank.

Ivan started to laugh, "I asked your dad if he'd allow me to take you with me. I told him that Aberdovey wasn't right for you, that if he allowed me to take you with me I would make something of you, you're special. Rightly so, he said you already *were* 'somebody', *his* son! And Billy you will always be his son. Ted and Emma love the both of you and the day you came into their lives was a blessing."

Billy started to smile, he was enjoying this story.

"I love you too, Billy, and I would have been just as proud to adopt you as the Talberts were. I wanted you to come to Edinburgh with me because I *know* that you will find yourself there. I'm happy you came after me because now I know that you made your own choice. We're going to have a great life in Scotland, but there is one thing I do insist on and it's non-negotiable."

Billy was dreading his next words. "You write to your parents every week – without fail, you never forget what they have done for you and you never ever forget your sister! You will go to school – there is a school purely for art students," seeing Billy's confusion, he explained further. "There is an art school in Edinburgh. It's for art students – obviously, dance, drama, singers, the whole caboodle, and it's where I want to try to enrol you."

Billy was speechless. It sounded like heaven! It was everything he loved to do. He would be in class with likeminded scholars, he wouldn't be teased or ridiculed or picked upon just because he didn't aspire to be a miner or a farmer, like his dad.

The train wheels rhythmically sang, 'I think I can, I think I can, I think I can' and as Billy listened to the sound of the train, he vowed it would be his motto – 'I think I can, I'm sure I can, I know I can'.

They opened up the rest of the bread, ham and cheese, stuffing it into their mouths, looking out of the window at the glorious countryside. The vast fields full of rape was spectacular.

"Look at that patch of yellow, over there, Billy. Isn't it beautiful?"

Billy nodded. It was. 'A patch of yellow'. He would remember this train journey with Ivan, his best friend, forever. He would never forget the smell or the taste of the fresh bread they bought from the baker, that morning. The realisation after hearing August Mensah's apologies that he was still a 'foundling' with no kin in the whole wide world to call his own, apart from his sister, Marley.

He suddenly had another faint memory of yellow. A yellow cardigan and being sick in a fast-moving vehicle.

'I love you too Billy. You're special.'

The train arrived at Waverley Station. Edinburgh.

Chapter 18: A New Start

Hank Ralston was the biggest, ugliest, most intimidating character Billy have ever encountered! He bore several facial scars, including at least a week's growth, part of his ear missing, a disfigured nose which one would presume he had broken at some time, a missing bottom tooth and arms full of crude tattoos. His frame was powerful, muscular and he was well over six feet tall. He greeted Ivan like a great bear hugging a sapling, knuckling him on the forehead, laughing with gusto while Ivan squirmed underneath, kicking out with his 'good' leg. Billy was dumbstruck and somewhat afraid, praying that he would not have to endure the same kind of welcome.

"Is this him, the great, wonderful laddie you have high hopes for, eh? A bit of a Nancy-lad like yourself is he? Aye, you've brought him t'the right place to make a man out of him, y'have an' all," Hank said, laughing like a drain, eyeing Billy at the same time.

"Ignore the brute, Billy, he's a pussy cat really. Hank, yes, this here is young Billy. I've already forewarned him that you're no gentleman, no need for the confirmation."

Hank roared with laughter and slapped Ivan round the head then gently approached Billy, scrutinising him . . . "hmm, definitely Scottish blood runs through his veins I tell ye. Look at those freckles and his red hair. Hahahaha, no Welshman could produce this colouring. By hiney the boy's more entitled to be here in the motherland than you! Billy! Are you gonna give your all t'Scotland, or what? We don't like losers here, boy!"

Billy had disembarked the train only moments earlier. They had had a long and tiring journey, one that he'd felt would be forever an unforgettable one. He was tired, confused, overwhelmed and yet he felt he had to acknowledge Ivan's 'friend' and be friendly, accommodating, but his wherewithal was ebbing . .

"Mr Hank," he spoke clearly and precisely, "I do intend to give my all. If I lose, it is not by choice, it means I have been beaten by something out of my control."

Hank's eyebrows raised slightly . . .

"Ivan has been very supportive throughout my life and I hope I don't disappoint him, myself or my family. I don't want you to get the wrong impression of me either."

It seemed he had certainly done just that! Neither he nor Ivan could muster any appropriate reply.

Hank walked with them from the train station to show them where he had secured accommodation for them in Buccleuch Street, talking ten to the dozen, firing questions and seemingly never giving Ivan time to answer. It was a couple of rooms above the boxing gym he ran, within a comfortable walking distance from Princes Street. Hank owned the whole block, his gym on the ground floor, his own flat on the next, and more rooms above that Ivan and Billy would use, for, as Hank had told him, as long as they wanted.

He was a very unlikely choice of 'friend', Billy thought, and felt sure he would, over the course of time, learn the reason why. For now, if Hank was a friend of Ivan's, that was all he needed to know.

Hank pushed open the door to the gym, allowing Ivan and Billy a sneak preview of the interior. Billy looked up at Ivan who was smiling from ear to ear, stepping over the threshold. A couple of things hit him immediately; one was of young boys his age, and others of around Ivan's age, all working out, dressed in oversized shorts and grubby white vests, sweat covering their bodies as they pounded away at punch bags hanging from ceilings, their concentrated faces never leaving their target. A couple of boys were sparring in the ring while another was throwing a medicine ball onto the stomach of one of the older lads as he lay on the floor, his stomach muscles rippling. The smell of rubbing oils and body odour was overpowering albeit in an intoxicating way. The walls were plastered with aged and cigarette smoke-discoloured bills displaying previous promotional boxing tournaments, photographs of boxers throughout the years, boxing gloves hanging from hooks, a couple of posters showing scantily clad women wearing bright red lipstick with pornographic graffiti scrawled upon that Billy found embarrassing to stare at.

They walked up the two flights of stone staircases until Hank unlocked the door to their new home. It was dingy and sparsely furnished, offering nothing of the warm ambience of Trefellon, but it mattered not. This was an exciting adventure for them both and as they glanced around, Hank said "welcome home brother, now get sorted quickly cos Ma Ralston is waiting to see you and meet the wee lad so don't be keeping her waiting. You've forty minutes, meet me downstairs."

Billy was loving listening to Hank; his Scottish accent was mesmerizing and it was making him feel uplifted, though he had no idea why. He felt he could listen to his chatter all day long.

There were two bedrooms so Ivan chose the larger of the two and showed Billy into the smaller room that was to become his. There was a bathroom which was simply astonishing as Billy had only ever known the tin bath that hung outside, brought into the kitchen once a week in which the whole family bathed in, in front of the range. An inside, flushing, toilet too! No more using the 'gozunder' or going outside in the dark to the thunderbox, having to encounter spiders and silverfish and all other kinds of creepy crawlies, let alone that smell! Scotland was already proving far more futuristic than Wales. He wondered what had prevented Ivan for so long from returning here.

"Tomorrow I'm going to send your parents a letter, Billy, telling them what happened and where you are."

Billy's face showed his concern, "don't worry, nobody can make you do anything you're not happy doing. "

He sat down on the little two-seater old leather settee in the small living room area, patting it for Billy to join him. "This is a new beginning for us Billy lad but you are free to go back to Wales, to your parents, anytime, if that is what you want. I will never stand in your way. But... and I have to explain to you so I hope you will understand why I *wanted* you with me, is... see, I know that you will benefit by being here, like I did. You will have a wider circle of friends, better support and encouragement to spread your wings."

"I want to go and pee," Billy said, desperate to use the modern toilet.

"Go, I've said enough."

Forty minutes later the two Welshmen once again stood inside Hank's boxing gym. Neither had had the opportunity of bathing or changing clothes, not that Billy

146

had a spare change of clothing; something Ivan had decided on doing the next morning. 'Ma Ralston' was expecting them for dinner that evening and she was not one who would take too kindly to being rebuffed!

The Ralston family home was in Fauldhouse, a fair trip in Hank's old not-so-legally-roadworthy jalopy. Nevertheless, when they pulled up outside the tiny two-up, two-down cottage, it had seemed worthwhile once they all savoured the delicious smell of cooking coming from inside.

Jean had heard Hank's car pull up and hurried out of the back door before her brother had the chance to hold her back, as he usually loved to do so. She was the elder sister of three and the Ralston brothers were extremely territorial over *all* their sisters; a trait endearing maybe, unless you were a sister of the brothers! Hank and Dougal, the two eldest brothers, were a nightmare. The minute either of them realised their sister, Jean, was going to meet a boy they would demand being fed: 'another piece of toast, Jean,' one would say, and she would never *dare* object! Her mother simply ignoring the protests – her boys were her diamonds and were refused nothing!

Jean loathed her bully-brothers, they stifled her freedom, and potential boyfriends feared getting involved.

Jean had been dating a lovely, kind and caring young man, Malcolm, and had managed to keep him a huge secret . . so far. Hence, when she heard that Hank was coming over for dinner, she did her utmost to ensure she was out. Tonight was a major success, she'd managed to escape!

Billy was totally surprised to find Ma Ralston was nothing like he imagined! She was tiny, about five feet in height and long greying hair tied at the nape of her neck in a tight bun. She wore a floral apron over a knee-length brown dress. She had a sharp face, a pointed nose and chin, making her look almost witch-like. Hank towered over her like a giant bear. She was genteel too, and that took Billy aback, he was expecting Hank's mother to be as formidable as he! But on the contrary, she was lady-like, petite, and everything in her little two-up, two-down was immaculate! The table was laid out for five people, there was a small vase of flowers on the table, a water glass at every place setting with a serviette in each, and a jug of water in the centre next to the flowers.

Ma Ralston greeted Ivan with much enthusiasm, "welcome back, son, it's good to see ye again, so it is. And the wee lad of yours - Billy is it?" she asked, nodding in Billy's direction, "and you're the dancer they tell me?"

Billy was surprised to learn that she had heard about him! "I do like dancing, yes. I also love that smell, what is it?" he said, looking towards the cooker, "it smells like steak and kidney pie."

"Snake and pigmy pie, Billy. Dougal couldn't say 'steak and kidney when he was a bairn, so it will always remain 'snake and pigmy'. DOUGAL . . . ." she shouted upwards, and seconds later another huge Ralston male appeared at the table!

The steak and kidney pie was - without doubt - the best Ivan had ever eaten! Billy was dithering over his food, he didn't eat meat but hadn't the heart to say anything for fear of causing offense. He carefully picked out the meat and left it on the side of his plate. The gravy with the mashed potatoes, however, tasted divine and Billy was falling asleep at the table; he'd had a very long day.

149

Back at Buccleuch Street, Hank carried Billy up the steps to their rooms and dumped him on his bed.   He bid goodnight to Ivan and left them, promising to meet up in the morning and reconvene for their discussions.

Hours later, the bakers, just a few doors away, would be at work making the soft rolls, the bread, cakes, pastries etc for the coming morning. Ivan would wake to the smell of fresh bread wafting upwards; it took all of his strength not to go downstairs and buy some and snuggle back inside the warmth and comfort of his eiderdown with the promise of at least another couple of hours' sleep before tackling – head-on, their new odyssey.

"Ivan! Ivan, wake up. There's someone at the door."

Chapter 19: Back at Trefellon

Ivan and Billy had been gone for over six months and Ted still hadn't managed to calm down. He was constantly 'chomping at the bit' with Ivan and angry that Billy had decided to run off to join him, disappointed to realise the boy loved Ivan more than he and Emma and couldn't imagine why on earth he would feel happier leaving his sister behind. Ted felt personally responsible, that he had let everyone down and his relationship with his wife was suffering.

There had been many an occasion when he wanted to pack a bag, jump on a train to go and find them, give Ivan a large and unpleasant piece of his mind, but he had no idea where to look for them. Edinburgh was a big city!

He had had to suffer the indignation of informing Billy's school teachers that he had moved to another area. He forced a smile to neighbours, reassuring them that it was a harmonious decision and all was well - when deep inside his heart broke.

Emma, Ted felt, was ambivalent. She hadn't appeared to be as upset, worried, or indeed as angry as Ted. She *knew* how close the two of them were, how much Ivan loved their boy and he would do everything he could to ensure his wellbeing, she had no doubt, but nonetheless, Ted would not be pacified.

They received the telegram Ivan had sent but Ted was not totally convinced of the short lines, feeling that in some way Ivan had manipulated Billy into joining him. A week later they received quite a lengthy letter from Ivan and a short note from Billy. Ivan had gone into more detail, explaining that he had got Billy into school and he was doing very well. He also described, on an extra page, their meeting with August Mensah.

He had been very reluctant to further Ted's angst by informing him of their encounter, but he felt they should both be aware of the possibility that neither child had been *legally* adopted. He was sure that Ted would construe this as his excuse to take Billy and cause him even more duress. He couldn't do right for doing wrong.

He never included a forwarding address on his letters.

Marley was now in school and she hated it! She had a tantrum every morning when Emma tried to get her ready, brush her hair, put on her dress, her socks and shoes. She wanted to stay at home and help her dad with the animals claiming that she could already read and write, she didn't need to paint pictures of houses or trees because she could see them every day. She knew that nine and seventeen made twenty-six because she could count. She had books, lots of them and read exceptionally well for her age. Marley was at her happiest when she was helping out on the farm, feeding the animals, collecting the eggs, she wanted to become a veterinarian – at five years old!

Emma had always felt that the two siblings were opposites and it was becoming more and more obvious. It looked as though it was going to be Marley who would become the biggest asset to Trefellon, but Ted was still not convinced. She was a girl, and girls didn't become farmers or veterinarians. Girls grew up to want fancy clothes, make-up, boys, marriage, children.

And so every morning, it was the same dilemma for Emma.

Boo had turned thirteen. Still ran around like a puppy dog but one day while they all sat around the breakfast table, she appeared to go into spasm. All four legs twitched and kicked out and her tongue lolled from the side of her mouth, her eyes were wide open and her body shook. Everybody leapt from the table and knelt beside her, Marley caressing her head and kissing her. Ted knew that it must be coming up to 'her time' though the thought filled him with dread. Boo had been the best of the best and he couldn't imagine their lives with her, he couldn't imagine not having her around.

Marley, steadfast in her love for the dog, refused point blank to go to school that morning, declaring that she was needed to comfort Boo. Neither Emma nor Ted refused her and so Marley spent the whole of that day curled up beside Boo, stroking her and talking to her, and occasionally trying to get her to eat a little food – which she refused.

Boo took her final breath at six p.m. that evening and Ted rose from his chair to go outside to the barn. He took up his shovel and began to dig a grave at the back of the barn, tears streaming down his face. Emma joined him, standing at the side, a torch held high, her face also wet with tears; Boo had played a huge part in their lives and had been worth her weight in gold.

Marley had attempted to drag her, using the corners of the crochet blanket she lay on to pull her outside to her grave. "Don't drag her Marley, please – don't drag her. Here, let me. I'll carry her."

Ted crouched down and wrapped Boo up in the many-coloured squares of the crochet blanket, whispering into her ear as he picked her up and walked over to the hole he had dug. He lowered her into the grave and stood for a minute or two, just looking down at her. Emma wrapped her arms around Ted's shoulders and they turned to look at one another, "thirteen years Em, remember? That ball of black and white fluff?" he managed to chuckle.

"Mmm, like it was yesterday, Hon. The cat left home that day."

They all stood around solemnly for a minute or two more before Ted broke away from Emma's embrace reaching for the shovel and began piling the black earth on top of her.

Tomorrow, he told himself, he would plant a shrub, a tree, something . . . on top, so she would always be remembered.

Marley went upstairs to her bedroom. It was all hers now and she had the whole bed to herself. She had a dressing table with a mirror on the wall, she had a pretty, musical jewellery box that when the lid was opened, revealed a beautiful ballerina in a white tutu and red ballet shoes. This is where she kept her brother's letters and now she wanted to hear his voice via his words. She loved to receive his letters and felt very grown up when the postman announced he had a letter especially for her!

She kept a little diary that she wrote in, everyday things that she would have liked to talk to her brother about. She didn't feel sad that he was no longer there, but there were occasions when she would have liked to talk to him, in person.

She had no understanding of why he wasn't with the family any longer, other than he had gone to Scotland with Ivan.

She wrote in her 'diary' to Billy that night as she did often, *'Boo died tonight Billy. She has gone to join all the angles in heven. Mum and dad and me all cryed. Dad berid her behind the barn, he rapt her in that colored blanket that uste to be on your bed. I hope yor having a nice time at school. I hate school! I want to be a vet when I'm old so I can luck after all the animals. P.s. What is lookeemia? Mandy at school says dad has it. Her dads a docter, that one that came to the hose when he bort one of are lams. By by for now. Marley moos.*

Ted lay awake for ages that night, too sad after the evening's events to close his eyes and sleep.

Emma came downstairs to sit in front of the range, a pile of letters in her lap that she wanted to reread.

Marley was fast asleep.

Elsewhere, Ivan, Hank and Dougal sat downstairs in the boxing gym in Buccleuch Street, going over the plans for Ivan's endeavour.

It was late, gone ten p.m. but the men were buzzing with enthusiasm and anticipation. Whatever Ivan wanted the

Ralston's were going to have to back him one hundred percent, even though it was way out of their imagination. He was their 'brother' and Ma Ralston would never allow them to *not* support him, whatever his aspirations - or foolhardiness!

Chapter 20: Pocket Money

"Ivan, can I please have some pocket money?" Billy asked.

Ivan was hand-washing their smalls at the kitchen sink and stopped at Billy's words. "Pocket money? Well, yes I suppose so, but what do you need pocket money for?" he asked.

"Erm, stamps for my letters."

"I post your letters."

"Well, I'd like some pocket money for . . . things."

"Billy, tell me what kind of 'things' and we'll agree or not on pocket money. You can go to the gym any time you like for free, it's just downstairs and Hank is more than happy for you to go, which, incidentally, you'd better get ready pronto because he's got a sparring partner for you to try out. Now then, what else?"

"I think I should have sixpence pocket money so that I can buy comics and cigarettes, and maybe . . ."

"Cigarettes! Are you having a laugh Billy lad? No no no no. Have you ever seen Hank or Dougal or me with a cigarette? Forget it. The answer is no. You can have pocket money if you can give me a valid reason why you need it. In fact . . . I tell you what, yes you can have pocket money, but you are going to have to earn it!"

He threw a pair of wet soapy underpants at him, "your presence is needed downstairs!" Billy ducked, the wet y-fronts smacking into the wall with a sopping plop, and headed down to Hank's gym.

Hank was in the corner of the boxing ring talking with a tall lanky kid about ten years old. He had greasy dark hair and his skin was ghostly white, looking no more a fighter than Billy felt, yet seeing the boy almost gave him a feeling of superiority. Hank spotted Billy's arrival and beckoned him into the ring, "ah, here he is. Billy this is Norman. I'd like the two of you to spar for a round or two, see how the pair of you get on. Norman's got a fight scheduled in a couple of weeks, just the usual amateur three two-minute rounds. He needs some practice and so do you. Glove up and come up here."

Billy spent hours and hours in the gym, he loved it equally as much as he loved his dancing lessons – when he had the opportunity. He could never decide which he preferred.

His dancing enabled him to soar, to be himself in ways that the gym didn't. It was liberating to dance across the room as a free spirit but that situation didn't arise too often as primarily it was routine barre work. The gym enabled him to develop his strength and muscles, and colleagues were on hand to encourage and nurture him.

Billy gloved up, as Hank requested. He took time applying the bandages to his hands before putting on his gloves, hoping Norman was watching and perhaps anticipating he was in for a thrashing. Billy was never going to be any pushover, he may appear just as nerdish as poor Norman, but poor Norman was going to have to work hard to get one over on Billy!

Gloved up, he stepped into the ring. "Touch gloves and walk to your corners," Hank said. "Dougal, you're with Billy".

The sparring was subtle for the first two minutes with both boys sussing each other out. Norman's long fringe kept falling over his forehead and he kept knocking back his head, flicking his hair away. Billy saw this miniscule lapse of concentration as his cue to jab on his jaw, following with a left uppercut to the side of his head, causing

Norman to totter. He maintained his stance, dancing from left to right and Billy almost laughed at his comedic attempt at portraying himself as a boxer, determined to show him exactly how to dance and box at the same time.

As Norman steadied himself, positioning himself in the prolific boxer's stance, Billy leapt around him like a young gazelle, circling him, teasing him with a few theatrical punches, his arms stretched out wide, feet on tiptoes enacting the 'pas das chat' he had learned at his dancing class, then kicking up his right foot almost flicking Norman's ear before landing in readiness for his next move, but Dougal was not impressed, he bellowed out in fury! "What the hell is this shambles Bill, you're supposed to boxing not taking the bloody mickey. Stop yer silly shenanigans and get outta here."

Billy stepped out of the ring, feeling somewhat smug. In fact, quite uplifted considering he'd actually achieved something out of the ordinary - to upset one of the Ralstons. He knew without a doubt Ivan would have loved his performance and cheered him on with loud whistles of encouragement. He could picture him laughing in his corner, shouting out advice to him and he would love to be able to run upstairs there and then to tell him all about it, but he knew he wouldn't have to; Hank would break his neck to do so.

Unlike his sister, Billy was enjoying his new school much more than when he was in Wales. It was full of boys and girls all more or less the same age and all anxious to show the world their talents, be it singing, dancing, or acting. There was no bullying because they all had the same agenda, they were encouraging and groups would congregate to discuss ways to improve themselves, exchange ideas, work together.

The premises next door to Hank's gym on Buccleuch Street became available to lease. It had been empty for six months with the previous tenant taking his retirement from his failing apothecary business; deciding to move back to the Shetland Isles where he still had a small croft. His son had been running the business during his war deployment, he being unable to conscript due to his 'mental health' status; however there were many that doubted his proclaimed incapacities!

The locals tolerated 'Patch' Irving, (the obvious nickname given to him due to the black eye patch he sported) tyrannical and brusque as he was, but they abhorred his son even more so. He was arrogant, belligerent and 'creepy' some said, but knew his stuff and they had no alternative than to patronise him. There was a big sigh of relief from all when they left.

Hank had already made the necessary enquiries about the lease for the premises, knowing Ivan's plans to open a bar for entertainment purposes. The former apothecary establishment was ripe for his endeavour. The counter would remain in situ to form a bar, with the optics behind. The false ceiling could be removed to install a stage for his dancers. Hank had many contacts and none would *dream* of refusing to help out.

A bonus factor was that it was literally next door to the gym and not a long walk from Princes Street. There was nothing else in the vicinity that would attract punters inside, to have a drink, be entertained. It was going to be something entirely new, alluring, different, and hopefully - money-making!

Dougal was very enthusiastic. He pictured himself leaving the gym and nipping 'next door' for a couple of 'swift halves' or more and crashing out in either Ivan's place or the gym! Ivan tried to explain over and over that *his* establishment was going to be so much more than just 'a pub'! His bar staff, for example, were all going to be male. The cabaret acts were all going to be male, but the singers and other acts could be both male and female.

Ivan was going to put Buccleuch Street on the map, a place where punters could come to be entertained. This had been his life-long dream and the Ralston brothers were one hundred percent on-board to make it happen for him at the insistence of not only Hank and Dougal, but Ma Ralston too! Ivan could do no wrong as far as she was concerned. She owed her all to him and loved him equally as much as her own bairns.

Billy was being included in all the negotiations and he was becoming more and more excited every day, wanting to see the whole thing into fruition. His demands for pocket money never wavered however, explaining that he needed a sixpence here, a shilling there to pay for the advertising posters he was getting one of his art colleagues to produce. He was trying to conjure a name for their place and wanted to surprise Ivan with a brilliant idea, up to now he hadn't. 'Ivan's Bar' didn't really do it, he knew the way that Ivan's mind worked and that he'd want something to encourage all walks of people to come and be entertained. It had to have an entertainment element in its name.

And then out of the blue, as Billy and Norman were talking after a session at Hank's gym, Norman said "call it 'Lifters' cos it's next door to this gym where everyone does some weightlifting, and it's gonna be run by a shedload of shirt-lifters. Seems the perfect name in my opinion."

"Shirt-lifters? What are shirt-lifters?" asked Billy.

Norman sniggered, "you'll know, sooner or later. Ask your dad," nodding towards Ivan.

Billy looked across at Ivan. 'Dad?' Is that who Norman thought he was? He wasn't about to enlighten him but he did like the idea of 'Lifters'. It was different, catchy, and he couldn't wait to tell Ivan and the others.

Hank roared with laughing! "Billy that is the funniest, best idea I've heard in years. It's bloody perfect, Ivan! Lifters! Hahahahahaha. Oh my God, you're gonna be stormin'. I wish I'd named the gym that instead of 'Hank's gym'! It's apt, it's different, it's staying! Dougal, get that mate of yours to make the signage, pronto. We're in business; hey Billy did you think of that yourself?"

Billy wanted to concede he had, but it hadn't been his idea, it was Norman's and even though he was very *very* tempted, he had to declare the truth, that it was Norman who had made the suggestion. His 'Bar Bizarre' idea seemed to have fallen on deaf ears.

Hank said that he was going to speak with Norman and give him a couple of shillings for his brilliant idea. God knows he and his family could use it, two shillings would be a great help.

Norman had been coming to Hank's gym since he was roughly about six years old, at Hank's insistence. He wasn't a brau laddie at all, in fact he was quite a paltry looking thing, inheriting more of his poor father's attributes than his wonderful mother's. Hank had been terribly sweet on Anne, Norman's mum, many moons ago but she was demure, lady-like and petite, whilst Hank was coarse, huge in stature and far from being a 'gentleman'. Her mother disapproved of Hank's visits to Anne and frowned upon any liaisons, ultimately steering her towards the more stable and respectable Claud Morrison, a local bank clerk in Civvy Street before joining the Royal Artillery; and now another casualty of the Second World War.

"I don't think I'm altogether keen on 'Lifters' Hank. It doesn't respectably portray what I have in mind. It seems crude to me, pathetic even, and I actually prefer something like 'Bar Bizarre' that Billy suggested, or 'The Candy Bar'; both depict everything I'm endeavouring to present. No, sorry, you can tell Dougal to tell that *mate* of his," he said sarcastically, "to cancel the signage. I'm still undecided."

And with that, he got up and walked away, leaving Hank with his huge mouth agape!

Chapter 21: Planning the Reunion

Even though restoration works were underway for the new venue, Ivan had still not decided on a name, going over and over all the suggestions. He and Billy had moved in and now they had their own living accommodation. They had a small but adequate kitchen with a gas cooker, sink, a little table and two chairs. Two bedrooms, a bathroom (with a toilet *and* a bath!) and a living room. Billy had the smallest bedroom that had a window overlooking the whole of Buccleuch Street and he would often gaze outside watching the early morning risers go to buy their bread from the bakers, dog walkers making their way down to Princes Street Gardens. It was a busy road and a huge difference to the vast open countryside of Wales, he loved it.

He found the whole renovation works exciting and would be astonished at the progress the workmen made every day when he returned from school.

Keeping his promise to Ivan, Billy continued to write letters to his parents and sister telling them of his new life and how he longed to receive news back. He understood

Ivan's reluctance to include their address, knowing Ted would race post-haste up to Edinburgh and demand his return, and that is something he didn't want to debate. He would feel terribly guilty at times, knowing the upset his departure must have undoubtedly caused but he could not bear to be apart from Ivan.

He had made good friends at school too, he felt liberated.

Dancing classes were his favourite. It was a mixed class of both boys and girls and primarily they were taught ballet. He didn't consider for a moment it was 'girlie' as there were ten boys and ten girls, and it was damned hard work every single lesson!

Madame Thirlby, the dance teacher, was frighteningly formidable, she rarely smiled or gave praise, no matter how hard they all tried to please. The class always began the lesson with barre work, then formed lines to practise adage, etc.

Being at the gym helped him no end in developing his timing, strength, stamina and muscles. Dougal never let up on him either, pushing and pushing, teasing and teasing, but he never retaliated, knowing it was just his ploy to rile him.

Billy didn't care too much for contemporary ballet, though, he preferred the classical and had high aspirations for himself.

Madame Thirlby was secretly very impressed with him, always performing to the best of his ability, she had no doubt that he could be a great dancer – if that was the path he chose because she knew that his mentors were male-orientated and wasn't sure if they were as fully supportive as if he had a female influence in his life. She knew Billy was totally in charge of his own destiny as she found him to be one hundred percent focused on everything he set out to do. 'If that boy had wings, he could fly' she told herself.

Academically, he was nothing out of the ordinary. His arithmetic was poor, his English was average (barely), his French was excellent. In other subjects he was mediocre, not really showing much interest in anything other than his dancing and his boxing. An odd combination, Madame Thirlby pondered, but nevertheless it worked. She

171

couldn't disagree that his time spent at the gym improved his dancing capability.

Madame Thirlby had a soft spot for Ivan too, her husband being in a similar situation – physically. Fred Thirlby had also taken a shot in the leg during his war years but then gangrene had set in and he ended up losing the whole of his leg.

She admired Ivan for the 'fatherly' role he had taken on with Billy; she had heard the gossip, of course she had, but was surprised to learn that they were not blood related; they were so much alike!

Billy walked into the kitchen where Ivan was leaning over a pot bubbling away on the gas ring. He was making a vegetable stew and he had bought some bread rolls from the bakers to go with it. The little table was laid ready, "Billy, how do you feel about participating in a boxing match? Hank thinks you're ready for your first fight. He has a tournament in mind and wants you in on it."

"Will I get paid?" he asked after a second or two's consideration.

"No, you won't! It's amateur boxing, amateur boxers don't get paid. Even professional boxers don't get a lot of money, until they're well-known."

"No, then." He answered.

"What do you mean 'no, then'? He's depending on you! He's got someone he feels will be a suitable match. It will be good for you to start getting noticed. It will be a brilliant night, you'll love it."

Billy went quiet for a few minutes, contemplating his next statement.

"Can my mum and dad come to watch me then? I haven't seen them for ages and I can't even receive a letter from them. If I can write and ask them if they'd like to come and watch me . . I'll do it."

Ivan had not considered a request such as that but he totally understood Billy's feelings. It was natural that he would want his family here to watch him, he had so much to impart to them all.

He served out the stew into bowls, and as they sat eating, he felt some trepidation. Would Ted accept Billy's invitation to come and watch him? Would he be pleased to know that his son was being indoctrinated into the macho world of boxing? It didn't paint a pretty picture did it? He worried they would both feel he wasn't looking after him as well as they had done, taken him away from the country-life and embroiled him in an environment full of fighters and bruisers!

And most discerning of all, would he insist he return to Wales with them, afterwards?

Deep down Ivan knew that Ted wouldn't have been able to lay any claim on Billy, according to the babblings of August Mensah, almost admitting the non-legal adoption papers, but he didn't want to pile that questionable fact onto his shoulders. He would acquiesce and deal with whatever happened, as and when.

"Okay," he replied after a while, nodding half-heartedly "after you come back from the gym tonight the pair of us will sit down and write letters. They can all stay in Hanks other rooms, next door. We'll invite them."

Billy was overjoyed, he leapt off his seat and ran round to Ivan, throwing his arms around his neck, "thank you, thank you. Oh, I hope they come! I haven't seen Marls for years". (*It wasn't years, it only felt like years.*)

Norman sat on the bench tying up his boot laces, already dressed in his shorts and vest. Billy sat next to him and began to take out his kit. "Do you know who you'll be fighting in this charade Hank's putting on?"

Norman turned to look at him, puzzled, "charade? Why do you say that? It's not a charade, it's a boxing match. Yes, I do know who he's put me with and I know I can win, Billy. Hank wouldn't put us against anyone who could beat us, his reputation is on the line. This will be my third fight and I can't wait. Why? Aren't you looking forward to it?"

Billy shrugged, "then it is a charade if he's matching us with lads he knows we can beat, isn't it?"

Norman hadn't considered this.

"Will your mum be coming to watch you?" Billy asked Norman.

"She wouldn't miss. She doesn't really like boxing," he laughed, "wouldn't normally be seen dead in this kind of place," he said glancing around "but I'm all she has now, apart from my grandad. I think he's coming too."

Billy stripped off down to his underpants and began to slowly dress in his gym clothes. He wanted Norman to watch him, he wanted to show off his young muscular body, he wanted to make him be envious.

"My mum and dad might be coming to watch, too" he said.

That was the very first time Norman had ever heard Billy mention dual parents, he was slightly taken aback, "your mum and dad? I've never heard you talk about your mum before. Are they divorced then?"

"Mum and Dad? No! They live in Wales. My sister still lives there."

Norman was getting more and more confused, then he burst out laughing, "you are hilarious Bill, everyone knows you live next door with your dad."

Dear Mum, Dad and Marley Moos, I have got somethink to tell you. Sorry its all in one letter this time but I cant be bothered to do two, so this is for all of you. Can you please come and wach me box? Ive told you all about hank and hes bin teeching me and I have my first fight coming up. I only said Id do it if Ivan agreed to let you have are address so you can stay in hanks place next dore. Its ok thow. Edinburough is grate and I think you will like it but its not like Wales, well it is in some places but not ware we are. We have a good bakers a cross the road and it does lovely bread.

I love my school and I realy realy love dancing. Ive got some nice frends too and there dying to meet you all. I hat to have a tooth out last week because it was killing me, my breth smelt horrible but its ok now. Please come mum and dad. I miss you and Marley. How is Boo? I miss her too, give her a big hug and kiss from me. Are address is on the back.

Lots of love from your son Billy. XX

Ivan read Billy's letter to his family before he put his own page in the envelope. Those two little words, 'your son'. He felt a slight pang of jealousy, which he knew was pathetic, stupid. Billy had chosen to follow *him*, but it was an itch he couldn't scratch to relieve. He was acting like a petulant child and he needed to dismiss his negativity, move on and be the very person the lad had determined to aspire to.

He licked the envelope and wrote a return address on the back, as promised. He gave Billy the coppers to take to the post office for the stamp. It was three weeks until Billy's debut fight. Enough time, Ivan considered, for Ted to make plans.

Three days passed when Ivan received a telegram. It appeared quite foreboding at first, just the basics; time and date of arrival at Edinburgh station. Nothing more.

Billy was ecstatic, he couldn't wait.

Madame Thirlby, however, was alarmed at his newfound enthusiasm and made a special visit to Buccleuch Street to confront Ivan, convinced he'd been giving him purple heart tablets! She stood in the doorway trying to decide how to climb over the debris and building materials demanding to speak to the owner. Ivan greeted her kindly, smiling from ear to ear and ever-so-humbly bent over in a bowing gesture. "Madame Thirlby, enchanté."

178

She was aloof and came straight to the point, "are you giving your son purple heart tablets?"

Ivan was shocked at her proclamation. "What? No, what on earth would make you think such a bizarre thing?"

"Oh, don't patronise me young man! I know what all you boys had to do to alleviate the pain. I don't blame any of you but to administer it to such a young boy . . it's despicable! You should be ashamed of yourself!"

"Madame; have you not considered that Billy is high on his own adrenaline at the thought of having his family come to watch his debut fight next week?"

She looked askance.

"Billy's mother, father and sister are coming here. Yes, his whole family will be coming from Wales. Like you Madame Thirlby, I am just a mere branch of his growing tree, helping him become the person he will be. You too are one of his very important branches, Madame. Please don't chip away at it, you will be most disappointed."

She glared at Ivan, and suddenly all her angst and confusion melted. Yes, she had assumed, like others, that Ivan was Billy's father. They were so alike, but in

179

mannerisms only, nothing in resemblance. She suddenly felt very humbled and embarrassed, and no matter how much she proffered her apologies, she left, feeling very silly.

Chapter 22: They're Here!

Billy was up at five thirty a.m.; he hadn't slept much more than a wink for the whole week prior to their expected date of arrival! He had been counting the days, the hours, the minutes until he now found himself standing next to Ivan on the platform at Waverley Station. He was apprehensive, nervous, thrilled, constantly watching the station clock that was displaying the arrival of trains and he'd been to the toilet three times already!

He had had a bath the night before, he brushed his teeth and his hair before six a.m. and had put on his best trousers and shoes. He could not stop smiling as he paced up and down the platform. He'd begged Hank to get some flowers to put in his mother's room and he'd bought Marley a little doll in a plastic tube, she was wearing the traditional national Scottish costume. He also bought her a book of animals and a bar of soap that was supposed to smell of heather.

He'd informed Ivan that he intended to spend his time at Hank's place with his family because they would have so much to talk about and he didn't want to miss a second.

They could now smell the acridity of sulphur approach before hearing the screech of the train wheels. Billy thought back . . 'I think I can, I think I can, I think I can . . '

He looked up and down the carriages, anxiously waiting for the doors to open, "Marley!!!!!!!". She was the first to alight, Emma behind, then Ted. Billy ran towards them, sobbing, trying to catch his breath. He hadn't expected to feel this amount of emotion, this awful sense of loss. His little sister had grown and he'd missed it all. He suddenly wanted to be transported right back to Trefellon, with his family, Boo, and all the farm animals and if he had had a magic lantern that could grant him such a wish, he would be right back there, right now.

"Mum, Dad," he was laughing and sobbing at the same time.

Emma let go of Marley's hand and she stood in front of Billy, holding him out in front of her arms, studying him, then hugged him. Her eyes closed as she smiled from ear to ear.

Ted was piling up all their suitcases, reluctant to yet meet Ivan's eyes. "Welcome," Ivan said. "It's about a twenty-minute walk to our place or we could get a taxi?"

"A walk is fine. We've not a lot in our cases," Ted answered dismissively.

He looked dreadful, though heaven forbid Ivan should say so. He looked grey, thin, and worn out. As they left the station Ted began to struggle with the weight of the cases and just then a car pulled up. It was Davy, at last! The youngest brother of Hank of Dougal.

"Taxi for Buccleuch Street?" he grinned. Ivan laughed out loud.

"I think we're safer walking Davy. Last time I listened to you I lost this!" he tapped his leg.

Davy reached behind and opened the back door, "aye, and before that ye saved the whole damn lot of us, now shut up and get inside afore I change me mind. Missus, ye sit yerself right here next to me."

Davy was grinning like the proverbial Cheshire Cat the whole of the five-minute journey to Buccleuch Street. He didn't switch off the engine as he jumped from the driver's seat and started to take out the suitcases, plonking them on the pavement directly in front of Hank's gym.

"I hope ye enjoy ye stay here in Bonny Scotland, and if ye needs anything, anything at all, ma brothers here will let me know."

He waved his arm out of the window as he drove away. Ivan watched solemnly... certain he caught him looking back...

"Ted, you and Emma are going to be staying here, upstairs. We're right next door. Please excuse everywhere, it's all under construction, but do feel free to come and see, have a look around. Billy is going to stay wherever he decides, if that's ok with you two. He's been looking forward to your visit and wants to show you what he's been doing. His dancing teacher would also like you to attend one of his classes so that . . ."

"Yes, thank you, we're all incredibly tired right now," Ted interrupted, "we'd just like a cup of tea and a few moments to relax. Billy, show us the way."

Enthusiastically, Billy helped with all the suitcases as they ascended the staircase, chattering non-stop on every step, turning to look behind at his sister constantly.

Hank had gone overboard. He'd got the flowers for Emma and tidied the place up. He'd put toilet paper in the bathroom, ensuring it was facing the 'right' way. He'd cleaned under the toilet seat, too, something he would never have dreamt of doing in his own place, but he had had his orders to make a good impression.

He'd gone across the road to the bakers and bought a dozen fresh soft rolls. His mother had sent over a jar of home-made raspberry jam, two dozen eggs and a bowl of dripping. She had insisted Hank give the 'boy's sister' a stuffed otter that she'd been busy making especially for her. Ma Ralston loved otters, they were her favourite wild animal and she wanted 'the wee girl' to have her own, feeling sure she'd have never encountered one in Wales.

Indeed, she could not have given a better gift, she absolutely fell in love with it.

Marley had never heard of an otter before, let alone seen one, but when she picked it up she studied it, turning it over and upside down, bewildered. She wanted to know more about otters. Did they only live in Scotland, what was their purpose in life, what did they eat? Where could she expect to find one? She couldn't imagine an otter walking down the streets here, in Edinburgh! The very gift added to confirming her ambitions to become a veterinarian. There was so much to learn.

The Talberts had just over two hours to settle in and get ready before walking downstairs and entering Hank's Gym to the boxing show. They were dumbfounded to find themselves at the back of a very long queue of eager patrons all keen to get inside and were surprised at how electrifying the atmosphere was!

Emma had never been to a boxing match before and wasn't altogether sure it was a suitable venue for her family then all of a sudden, she felt herself and Marley being pulled from the queue and shoved at the front entrance!

The burly man holding on to her arm spoke to the man at the door collecting the money, "VIP guests, not too close, not too far away" and were escorted to some middle seats that had a bird's eye view of the ring. Emma and Ted shuffled uncomfortably in their seats, next to an attractive young woman and an older gentleman, while Marley brimmed with excitement at the prospect of seeing her brother up there. So far, she was thoroughly enjoying her visit to Scotland.

Ivan joined them, much to the chagrin of Ted who felt unable to revert to the camaraderie he had once shared with him. "He won't be on for a while yet Ted, but Hank's confident on a win. He's had various different sparring partners over the last few months so... fingers crossed an' all that, hey?"

Ted nodded, "I'm sure he can hold his own," he glanced at Ivan, "well, he's proved he's mature enough to make his own decisions after all."

"Ted! I swear to you I had no idea Billy would think of following me, you must know that. I would never have *taken* him, he's always been yours. But there he was, and I was not about to leave him there nor was I about to cancel my plans. As you say, 'he's mature enough to make his own decisions', and believe me he is and he does! It was his decision to write to you and invite you here. He wanted you all to be here to see him."

Ted didn't answer.

"He's a lucky lad to have so many people wishing to be his parents, when apparently his own didn't." Ivan left Ted to consider his words as he left his chair and walked away.

Norman climbed into the ring, seemingly oozing confidence. He was wearing red shorts and a matching red vest. His mum had been in the dressing room with him earlier, wrapping the bandages around his hands before he put on his gloves. It was an idiosyncrasy of hers to roll his bandages, meant to bring 'good luck' and it could only be she who applied them to her son's hands before a fight.

She sat apprehensively next to her father, Norman's grandad, her stomach doing somersaults, terrified at the prospect of someone hitting her boy when she had never so much as lifted a finger.

Dougal was in his corner, applying Vaseline to his forehead, his nose, and on his cheeks, constantly reassuring him and giving him advice, and then the bell rang, 'seconds away, round one'. She grabbed her father's hand and squeezed it tightly, but her father shoved it away and stood up, "go on our Norman, give him what for!"

Callum Stirland was also a local boy, albeit from a neighbouring gym, and he wasn't going to be anyone's doormat. He had five wins under his belt already and was looking for number six. He trained every single day, come rain or shine and was totally focused. He was also a southpaw, which Norman was going to find challenging!

He entered the ring dancing from left foot to right, holding his fists in front of his face, staring at Norman, while the referee introduced the two fighters to the audience.

Billy stood in the wings, watching. He surveyed the crowd, looking at their reactions and spotted his own family watching the scene.

He saw his stablemate take his first blow to the chin, making him stagger for a miniscule of a second. Callum gained confidence and followed through with a right upper

189

cut, catching Norman on his right ear. He fell, bringing him to his knees, his hand covering his ear.

The bell rang for the two-minute ending and both boys sauntered to their corners. Dougal was shouting expletives to Norman but he wasn't able to hear as he took a big swig of water, swilling it round his mouth and then spitting it into a bucket at his side. He looked around the faces, furtively seeking out his mother and his grandfather. He saw them. He saw their worried expressions and he didn't like it one little bit. He wasn't here tonight to disappoint his kinfolk, he was supposedly here to make them proud of him. He wasn't about to be beaten by the likes of Callum Stirland, he was here to win for Hank Ralston!

'Seconds away, round two.'

Norman leapt up from his corner approaching Callum Stirland, he didn't want to give him a chance to get another over him so he tore into him, pummelling his body, powerful body blows, punch, punch, punch. Callum took every punch, and opened his mouth wide, smiling tauntingly behind his slimy gumshield, sweat dripping from his forehead, and as he brought up his right fist to deliver a right hook, Norman delivered the devastating blow to the side of his face, spinning him headfirst to the canvas.

The referee knelt beside him, counting . . . three, four, five . . . then stood up and raised Norman's gloved hand in victory. He wasn't able to hear the cheers, the stomping feet, the whistles and shrieks. He wasn't able to hear anything at all.

He left the ring and walked back to the dressing room in silence. It was an eerie silence too - a strange, dull, numbness.

Billy was waiting back in the dressing room for him, buzzing with admiration, excitement, couldn't wait to welcome him back and wrap his arms around him in a hero's welcome and tell him how fabulous he looked out there, which he did, but Norman didn't appear to register anything Billy was saying. He could see his lips moving and could tell by his facial expressions that all had gone in his favour but he felt odd, distorted.

Hank appeared in the dressing room next, slapping Norman on his back telling him how proud he was of him, what a fantastic performance and that his mother would be over the moon, but all Norman would comprehend was two things. He was well aware that he'd won the contest, but he didn't feel the slightest bit euphoric; in fact he felt extremely discombobulated.

Callum Stirland walked into the dressing room seconds later, sullen and accompanied by his trainer. He saw Norman, Billy and Hank and walked over to them, grabbing Norman's hand, shaking it, "congratulations, Champ," he said, "you kicked my ass... this time. I want a rematch," he laughed "so I can pay you back."

"Bill," Hank said, "you're up next."

Billy glanced across at the unassuming Norman who looked as if he would fit more comfortably in a clerical environment than a boxing dressing room! He studied his own gloved hands and considered the impact the next few minutes would have on him and his opponent, his little sister and his parents who had travelled all the way from Wales to Scotland to watch his debut. Watch him do what, exactly? To fight! That is what the people had flocked to Hank's gym to see tonight, to watch boys and men fight each other. They got high on it. The thrill of watching a man destroy the person in front of him, the 'opponent', to draw blood, perhaps? To render him unconscious? Place monetary bets as to who was the better man? Exactly the same scenario as being at war just years earlier. Surely that was all part of the past? Humanity had left such violence behind so why was he even considering his next movements? For whom?

He removed his boxing gloves and told Hank he was ready. Hank howled with laughing, "bare knuckling boxing went out with the Ark Bill, get' em back on."

Billy winked at Norman, "see you in ten minutes - max."

The referee was standing in the middle of the boxing ring, pacing from foot to foot. Jimmy Watts was sitting in the blue corner, his demeanour relaxed until he saw Billy climb under the ropes, gloveless. He looked questioningly at his corner who shrugged his shoulders; it was unheard of. Billy looked around for his family and spotted Marley standing on her chair, he lifted his hand in a slight wave to her then took his seat in the corner. Dougal was not impressed. He offloaded a cartload of expletives to Billy who was totally ambivalent, smiling and gesticulating to all those standing around cheering. He should be feeling nervous, apprehensive. He'd watched Norman's fight and two previous others and this was, after all, his debut night!

In fact he felt no fear nor trepidation or anxiety whatsoever. He felt confident, excited and he was going to take centre stage! It was going to be his opportunity to fly.

Jimmy Watts had travelled all the way from Livingstone to be matched against Billy Talbert; a 'dead-cert' he was assured as Billy had never had a fight. Jimmy had had loads but never inside a boxing ring! Equally matched, then?

The bell rang. Both boys sprung up, meeting in the middle of the ring and touched hands. From that moment of the bell ringing, it was a right fiasco! A complete mockery of 'boxing' from Billy. He danced around Jimmy, making him look a complete fool. He jabbed his bare fists repetitively, rapidly, never making contact. He ducked and weaved, danced and taunted.

Billy was fast. He was fit, strong and nimble   He was a dancer, a boxer and a fighter, but never a killer and it was looking as though he wasn't about to become a winner either.

He slumped into his corner after the first round, feeling already defeated. He hadn't anticipated this at all, this exertion, humiliation. He was about to throw in the towel when he saw Marley there, standing down in the corner, smiling from ear to ear. "Billy you are brilliant. Mum and Dad are loving it. I hope you win." And then she was gone!

He knew he wasn't brilliant and he realised he'd just brought his family all this way to watch himself become a laughing stock, he was going to disappoint them – again! What had he done? Trying to be more holy than thou, that's what he'd done!

"Dougal, get me my gloves back. I'll try without them for now, I'm sorry." Dougal raised his eyebrows and rolled his eyes, relieved that Billy had seen sense.

'Seconds away, round two.'

Both boys walked towards each other and this time as boxers. The previous 'booing' had stopped as Billy squared up to Jimmy Watts, throwing the first bare-fisted blow to his body. Watts retaliated by throwing a jab, comically missing as Billy sprung sideways. For two minutes the boys captivated their audience in suspense.

When the bell rang, Ivan was waiting with Dougal in the corner with a pair of gloves. Billy put them on trying to explain his reasoning for going without. "Not now Bill, just get out there and do what you've come here to do. Think of it as sparring with Norman, like you do all the time," Dougal said.

He returned to a barrage of appreciative whistles and supportive heckles. He couldn't see the audience through the thick mist of cigarette smoke that filled the arena but he was now totally focused on his target, his determination and adrenalin oozing from his pores. He didn't have to be a killer but he could be a boxer, playing by the rules. He knew that Ivan had been in the war and hadn't killed a single person. He had gone as a soldier, a fighter, as a dutiful man. He had returned as a soldier, a dutiful man, and from the odd snippets of information he heard, a 'hero'? If Ivan was being hailed a hero without hurting a single enemy, so could he.

Jimmy Watts wasn't his enemy, he was merely an opponent, and an opponent that was about to become his first victory.

A perfect cross to Watts' face caused blood to pour from his nose, he winced and covered himself with his gloves. Billy saw his opportunity to throw hook after hook to the body, but Watts was not in a hurry to throw in the towel. With a bloody nose he purposefully pursued Billy, his expression murderous.

The bell rang, ending the fight and Watts glared at the referee, furious at being denied any more time.

The adjudicators unanimously declared Billy the winner and the punters were in obvious agreement. He was on cloud nine.

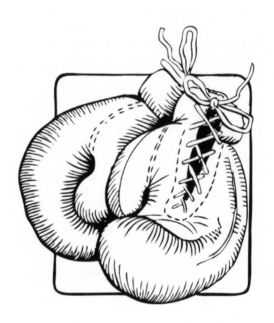

Chapter 23: The Telephone

The time was approaching for saying their goodbyes to each other. Ted claimed he could only manage to leave the farm for a short time with hired help but he was longing to get back to the glorious countryside of Wales and his comfortable bed!

Marley had told Billy about Boo's passing, of her absolute certainty that she was going to be a vet when she left school and was going to live in Wales forever. She missed him, she reassured him, but was happy to be able to come and visit. And now she had his address so they could write to each other all the time.

Emma was a lot more forgiving than Ted. She understood the reasons why Billy had gone in search of Ivan and knew that they would be good for each other.

Both Ted and Emma had been informed of the surreptitious actions of the unscrupulous August Mensah and were extremely dismayed. They knew they had no legal rights over either of the children but Marley was too young to make any decisions, beside which she had only ever known Ted and Emma as parents. They vowed to delve more meticulously when they returned, armed with their newly found knowledge.

Ivan desperately wanted to adopt Billy but hadn't dared broach the subject. He wasn't even sure he would be allowed, being a single man. He'd lain awake night after night trying to conjure up some believable story to make the authorities concede. It seemed incredulous that everyone already assumed he *was* his father!

The evening after the boxing match, Ivan invited Ted for a chat in the gym. There were no local pubs in the vicinity and Ivan wanted a clear head anyway. The gym was always a hive of activity, cussing and banter; besides, Ivan had plenty of moral support in the gym. He'd also had time to think of everything he was planning on saying. He would have preferred Emma's company too, but she had Marley and Billy for the evening.

Ivan gave Ted a conducted tour of the gym, pointing out the various pieces of equipment, drawing his attention to the many posters on the wall of previous boxing tournaments depicting well-known Scottish boxers, explaining the training procedures, extolling the virtues of the trainers. He told him about the school Billy attended, a theatrical-based school that concentrated on all art forms, dancing, acting, music, etc. He reminded Ted how encouraged the students were to be able to express and be themselves without the persecution from main-stream school students. Billy was free to emerge from his cocoon as himself.

Though Ted found it hard to let go, he had to agree that it was indeed the best thing for his son. Disappointed, yes, but he knew the truth deep down, he'd just had a hard time accepting it.

"Well, at least we know we have one thing in common," Ivan said, facing Ted.

"What's that?" he asked.

"A love for the boy."

Ted hung his head, feeling somewhat like Billy's opponent in the boxing ring, a loser - by unanimous decision.

"We're not at war here, nor are we fighting a battle; I'd like us to agree that we're both in his corner. So . . . Mr T," he smirked at the risk of using his previous term of endearment to his former employer, "what say we take *our* gloves off now and vow our unconditional support?"

"Like you said, we have that in common."

Ted shook Ivan's hand. Ivan leaned forward and hugged Ted, "you can be more proud of him than you can imagine. He can visit you whenever he wants to and, likewise, you are all welcome to come back and stay here any time. Any time at all."

Ted looked around the gym. To him it seemed a gloomy place, filled with the smell of stale sweat and rubbing oils, dirty socks and wet towels. Not so dissimilar after all to his very own sheep pen, the smell of damp wool when the sheep returned from being outside in the rain, the wet straw, the dipping solutions.

"I thought he might have taken on the farm. You know, after me. *Wished* he would have wanted to, rather."

Ivan nodded, awaiting and anticipating Ted's next statement, all the time waiting to make eye contact with him.

"Anyway, seems he's doing just fine here in Scotland, with you, that's something I don't have to worry about. Hmm.

I've been considering selling off our livestock, you know." Ivan didn't express any surprise.

"Boo's gone now, and I did consider getting another puppy, Em and I talked about it. Oh Marley would have loved one," he said, actually smiling now, "but to be honest Eiffion, sorry – Ivan, I feel I just wanna 'Angus me coat up'" he said laughing, "is that what you say up here? I feel like I'm slowing down now... nothing I would admit to Emma of course!" Ivan nodded in agreement.

"You'll let Billy know, everything... won't you?"

Ivan turned now and looked Ted in the eye. "I've never not done."

"So," Ted continued, leading the conversation away, "what name have you decided on for your future enterprise?"

"I've had so many suggestions, Mr T, good suggestions too, but I'm still in limbo."

"Ha, seems you already have your name then," he smirked. "In limbo. Inn Limbo?"

Ivan sat bolt upright as Ted began to reel off the many meanings, "in a forgotten or ignored place, orphaned children left in limbo... trying to decide what to do next... and he found himself listening, feeling and hearing the sound. Could Ted have nailed it? Were they all 'in limbo'? He was, definitely: *they* were! But being 'in limbo' was surely the beginning? And the beginning was just that! Great oaks grew from a single acorn. Beginnings, saplings, fledglings. He was interested. His world was about to burst forth into Inn Limbo. As a child he had been constantly 'in limbo' ignored and forgotten. In the war too and then upon his return to Aberdovey his life had been 'in limbo', it could not have been a more fitting suggestion. He said the words out loud, 'Inn Limbo' and the more he said it, the more he laughed out loud and the more convinced he became he had found it.

Davy suddenly appeared before them, totally unexpectedly and sat himself down in front of Ivan and Ted, grinning like a schoolboy. He'd come to find out when he was required to collect the Talberts to take them all to Edinburgh station. Ted stood up, putting his hands in his pockets, "I've always had a hankering to visit Prestonpans and Inverness and we're in Scotland, which I believe could be my children's birthplace, I'd like to extend our trip by a day or two and see a little more of your country. Davy, could you take us there, tomorrow?"

"Not until after ten in the morning, sir. Hank's having one of those new fan-dangled telephone things installed first thing, so I need to be here at the gym to make sure it's put in its proper place. After that, aye, I'm free," he replied.

Ivan and Ted looked at Davy, impressed, "Hank's having a telephone?" Ivan exclaimed.

"Says it's the 'way forward' and everyone's having them now. You'll do well to get one for next door too Ivan, when you get yerself sorted."

Ivan and Ted nodded, "how much does it cost? For the telephone?" Ted asked.

"Och, I've nae idea, sir. But ye ken a Scotsman doesn't part with his money easily, so I cannae imagine it's a lot. Ask our Hank."

The cogs were certainly working overtime in both Ivan and Ted's minds! A telephone would be a great lifeline for being able to keep in touch, and a hell of a lot quicker than sending a letter. It was something neither of them had given a thought about but now it made a heck of a lot of sense. Billy and Marley would be able to talk to each other whenever they wanted to, and so would Ted and Emma!

For the first time in many months, Ted actually felt some excitement. He wanted to know more about this 'telephone contraption', dismissing his previous conception that it was a total waste of money and would never 'catch on', feeling miffed that it had been a damned Scotsman to make him see it all so differently.

"I'd like to be able to be here to see it, if that's okay? I'm going to discuss the possibility with Emma, though I doubt she'll show any interest. Hmm, a telephone? Well, I've never considered myself blasé enough to think I know it all because something new comes along every day, doesn't it? Just look here for example, *you* have a toilet *inside* your house - and a bath! We don't, at Trefellon. We have an outside toilet that is emptied by the night soil men every Friday, and our weekly bath takes place in front of our range in the kitchen from the tin bath we have to bring indoors!"

Davy and Ivan stood side by side laughing at Ted, "Welcome to the twentieth century, old man."

(Ted's words spun in Ivan's head, 'I've never considered myself blasé enough to . . .' Blasé – he *liked* that word. He'd really only wanted one word for his club. In limbo was good and so was Inn Limbo but it wasn't going to be an Inn, he'd never considered offering overnight accommodation as that would entail a lot of extra money to be spent. Blasé was a great venue name and a five lettered sign was going to be a lot cheaper than any other alternative he'd thought about. He was going to ask Emma's opinion, even though his mind had been made up, at last!)

Ted was just about to leave the two men when Hank walked into the gym, his face distorted in concern, his shoulders slumped forwards and he plonked himself on the bench in front of the lockers, "I've just been to see Anne," he declared, shaking his head.

Ivan and Ted looked at each other in confusion, "Anne?" said Ivan.

"Norman's mum!" Hank answered, raising his voice, irritated that Ivan had had to ask, "Norman's in the bloody hospital for Christ's sake!"

"Norman? Why? What's wrong with him?" enquired Davy.

"Bloody perforated ear drum, that's what's bloody wrong with the lad. Callum Stirland landed him a right hum-dinger and the lad's ear drum's been damaged."

Poor Norman! Hank felt dreadfully responsible knowing that Anne was *never* going to forgive him. "What am I going to do?" he asked, looking at all the faces, looking at him.

"Hank," said Ivan, "is it perforated or ruptured? It happens, but after a while it usually mends with no permanent hearing loss. I remember a lot of our guys in France, they had the same thing when a bomb went off nearby. They'd scream in pain, holding their ears. Blood would pour down their necks. Couldn't hear a damn thing for weeks afterwards."

Just saying the words out loud and describing the situation to Hank transported Ivan back to the battlefields. The smells of decaying flesh, feces, and unwashed bodies. The sounds and percussion waves of exploding artillery shells. The agonised moans of the wounded and dying. Officers and sergeants barking orders, trying to be brave, but at the same time scared shitless just like the infantrymen.. It was the same every time, impossible not to, and he imagined it was the same for everyone who managed to make it back, alive. That's why so many never did talk about it. It was pushed to one of the back boxes in everyone's memory, but never being buried deep enough to allow total eradication, like a clawing parasite always trying to crawl to the surface, resurrecting its ugly head, taunting, persecuting, relentlessly.

Hank glared viciously at Ivan. "I put that boy in the ring with Stirland and I've got his goddamn mother hating every bone of my body and you tell me 'it happens', I *KNOW* it bloody well happens and I'm the one that *MADE* it happen!" his spittle flying in Ivan's face. Hank squared up to Ivan, his formidable stare never wavering, "and that's some consolation to his mother?"

"War time or peace time, Hank; friend or foe - shit happens," and Ivan walked away, out of the gym, leaving Hank to wallow in his own guilt.

Billy and Marley walked into the kitchen where Ivan was sitting at the table, stewing over Hank's verbal attack. They were boys, learning to fight in an organised manner, not out on the street or at war like many of a similar age, only years earlier. Boxing was a 'gentleman's sport' and all the youngsters were indoctrinated into practicing this very core rule. They were in the ring, not being wrapped up in cotton wool, but being trained to defend themselves, they weren't parading the streets being nuisances or thugs.

Soldiers were taught how to defend themselves but not like a boxer on a one-to-one basis. A soldier *was* taught to kill, with bayonets, bullets and grenades. Norman should consider himself lucky he was too young to experience the real world, a real wound, and an unreal 'battle'. Anne could be angry with Hank as much as she liked but she had a whole lot more to thank him for too.

"Uncle Ivan, we've come to kiss you goodnight," said a very smiley Marley hopping onto Ivan's lap, her arm around his neck.

"Goodnight Princess, sleep tight don't let the bedbugs bite," he kissed her back.

"When you and Billy come to Wales again how old will I be?"

"Well, let me think about that. You're twenty-three now, so... I think you'll be about twenty-four," he joked.

"I'm not twenty-three, I'm nearly six and did you know that when I'm old I'm going to be a vet so that I can look after all the animals on our farm and all the animals in the world?"

Ivan had no doubt that Marley would become the vet she aspired to be, but not at Trefellon; unless Marley did take on the farm, unless Ted didn't sell off his livestock, and unless Ted wasn't as ill as he looked!

"And your dad and I are going to get telephones, Marley, so that you and Billy can talk to each other any time you want to, all of us can."

"We have to go now, Uncle Ivan, we've got to go to bed. We're going to Pots and Pans and Inverness and I want to find some otters. That Davy man is going to drive us tomorrow on Saturday, and then the next day we go home on the train."

Chapter 24: The Trip

Unbelievably, the telephone had been installed in record time and by eleven a.m. everyone was eager to set off for their trip. Ted sat in the front passenger seat next to Davy while Emma sat in the back with Billy and Marley.

Inverness was over 150 miles away from Edinburgh so they had previously decided they would stay overnight somewhere close by, Ted insisting that he pay for Davy's accommodation too. Emma had packed up some food for their journey; soft rolls lathered with real Scottish butter, ten hard boiled eggs, five apples, a bag of tomatoes and half a pound of cheese.

Davy tossed a brown paper bag over his shoulder to Emma, "ye cannae come t'Scotland without trying our traditional haggis. It's brau, I tell ye, and incredibly hard to find this time of the year," he chuckled.

"Haggis? what's haggis?" asked Billy. It didn't look very appetising, it looked like minced up meat and he'd made everyone aware that he doesn't eat animals.

"Och, ye see a haggis is an extremely rare Scottish mountain beastie, Billy, that only comes out at night-time so it's incredibly hard to find 'em, and they can *only* be caught by putting salt on their tail."

Marley was enthralled, "will we be able to see some, Davy? I've never seen a haggis," looking at the sausage-like contents inside the paper bag. "I can't see its tail."

"Scotland has many curious beasties, hen. Have ye heard of our Loch Ness Monster?" Emma and the children gasped, none of them had any idea that monsters still existed, so Davy – once again, went into tourist-guide-mode enlightening them about Nessie, the sightings and proclamations, promising them a drive-by when they neared Inverness to see if they would be lucky enough to witness Scotland's historic 'monster'.

Ted sat smiling, listening to Davy tease his family.

They drove for miles and miles, and everyone was enjoying Davy's non-stop banter, the glorious Scottish lochs and glens, oohing and aahing along the way.

Ted had never been allowed to participate in the war and so was never able to justify his thoughts, alternating between feeling relieved and robbed at the same time. He wasn't therefore able to join in the camaraderie with veterans or add his two-pennyworth on any occasion, but that hadn't stopped him learning and reading all he could about all wars; it held a morbid fascination for him.

He was keen to see where the Battle of Prestonpans took place and the iconic Battle of Culloden between the Jacobite and the British Army. Prestonpans was in East Lothian and Davy explained that it wouldn't take too long to get there.

"You've known Ivan long?" enquired Ted.

Davy hesitated for a split second . . "I have, aye, just afore the war. We enlisted together."

Ted nodded, waiting to learn more but Davy seemed to stop talking; and then, "aye, a fine, fine man is Ivan," he said smiling, turning quickly to look at him.

"He's our brother-from-another-mother, a blood-brother you could say, and our Ma worships the very ground he walks on, we all do. In fact, I'd go as far as to say that there are a lot of mothers, wives and lassies in Edinburgh who feel exactly the same as our Ma."

Billy was listening to everything from the back seat and leaned forwards so that he could learn more.

"Ivan never talks about being in the war, Davy. Why do you think he doesn't? I tell him everything - my thoughts, my dreams, how my day at school has been, but he has never told me any war stories. Please tell us some more."

Davy concentrated on his driving, his forehead creasing in confusion, "we dinnae get many sheep shagg... many Welsh folk visit our Motherland and it's a pleasure indeed to have you all here. So, he's never telled ye? Och, I ken folk never de talk about it, it was nae picnic out there in France Billy lad, nae picnic at all and p'haps he never talks about it because it was just too horrendous to remember. But folk round here don't forget Ivan, or what he did - and what he didn't do either... aye Billy, some things are too raw, de ye ken?"

No, Billy didn't 'ken'. He didn't understand what Davy was saying, or implying, and neither did Ted or Emma. They never knew the reason why Ivan had been rumoured to be a hero.

Davy glanced around at Ted, then looked behind at his passengers in his mirror, seeing their confused faces, "he was awarded The Victoria Cross, you didn't know about all those men he saved?"

"Mummy I need to wee-wee," Marley announced!

"Time for a break I think," said Davy, slowing his car and driving into a little pull-in. A discrete hedge offered the ideal modesty screen for Marley – and Emma! Billy, Ted and Davy however were nowhere near as modest and relieved themselves as though in some urinary competition!

Prestonpans was nothing like Ted had anticipated, which wasn't a great surprise as the battle had been over two centuries ago, but nonetheless he felt deprived.

They unexpectedly came across a junk yard owned by a hefty old fella named Jock Black, notoriously rumoured to be a direct descendant of the one and only Charles Edward Stuart – the founder of the Jacobite Army (the 'Highland

217

Army' as was often referred to) and Jock lived in a humble, wooden structure that he called home, surrounded by 'junk'. It was a huge plot of land that had everything, for sale.

Davy parked the car, and everyone got out to have a look round. There was a magnificent grand piano under some type of tarpaulin as protection; several disused railway carriages with tables full of various pieces of China, pots, ornaments, candlesticks, chairs, furniture. Outside were swings, benches, locomotive parts and old motorcycles, prams.

Another carriage was full to the brim with dolls, both China and celluloid, spinning tops and toys of every description, sports equipment, medicine balls and punch bags, a wooden horse and yards and yards of thick rope that looked as though it would belong on a ship.

Everyone went off in different directions, scouring to find a keepsake to remember this day. Jock Black sat silently in his rocking chair, smoking his pipe and reading his Almanac, oblivious to any potential customers.

Billy and Marley walked together into the carriage containing the toys and sports equipment, Marley drooling over a stuffed owl she'd spotted in a glass dome, and she wanted to buy it. She could put it on her bedroom windowsill and study it every night, imagining it being alive and sitting in the apple tree where the swing was.

Then Billy noticed a box underneath one of the tables that was displaying a whole range of China teacups, saucers, teapots etc. It was a box that immediately reminded him of Hank's gym, that recognisable, unforgettable smell. He pulled out two well-worn and mouldy boxing gloves, two stinking boxing boots, a pair of sky-blue boxing shorts that looked bloodied. Yards of grey bandages that he recognised as the same kind of crepe bandages that Norman's mum applied to his hands before a fight. He peeked inside the burgundy leather boxing gloves and saw a name crudely etched inside . . . . *Benny Lynch*!

Benny Lynch! He took a sharp intake of breath; everybody knew Benny Lynch! Almost hyper-ventilating he picked up the box and ran outside with it, trying to find Ted.

"Dad," he cried out loud, "Dad, where are you?"

219

Jock Black stopped rocking in his chair after hearing Billy shout for his dad, he put down his Almanac and walked over to Billy, "a boxing fan are you laddie? And ye ken Benny Lynch? I'm impressed."

Billy was smiling from ear to ear, "a flyweight like myself, I've just had my debut fight on Friday night. I won too," he said proudly, "Benny Lynch was the best boxer in the whole world; we have pictures of him in our gym."

Jock sniggered, "aye, we all think that of Benny. Came from the Gorbals, ye ken, Glasgow. Sad story of the lad, so it is, the alcohol it was, ruined him and his reputation. I take it you don't partake of the demon drink?" he winked.

Billy looked indignant, "no sir! I don't!"

Jock Black studied him, running his eyes over his face, his form, the box he held in his arms, "a shilling and no less, and if ye decide to buy you make sure you do justice to the man who wore 'em afore ye." Then he left to go back to his rocking chair.

A whole shilling! He desperately wanted this box of Benny Lynch's boxing memorabilia, and he now had the dreaded prospect of asking his dad for the money! Marley's domed owl wouldn't be near as much as a whole shilling and he felt sure she would be able to wrap their parents round her little finger into purchasing her keepsake.

He considered asking Davy to sub him the necessary pennies until he could think of a way to pay him back, but it wasn't necessary as Emma had been watching from the side: she joined them. "Sir, you do know that my son here is the next potential Benny Lynch, do you not? His name is Billy Talbert, wait – let me write that down for you," she reached inside her handbag for a pencil and grabbed the Almanac Jock Black had been reading, writing on the back 'Billy Talbert was here, aged ten years old, equally fit to walk in Benny Lynch's shoes'. That sir, will be one shilling."

For the first time in sixty-five years, Jock Black had been rendered speechless.

"Hey Johnnie Cope are ye walking yet, or are your drums a-beating yet", Davy was singing away trying to get everyone to join in with him. The song was commemorative to the Battle of Prestonpans and most, if not all, Scotsmen knew it. The Scots were proud of their history, and this was the whole purpose of the trip, especially for Ted, to see some of it.

He'd never tasted whiskey either and he had a yearning to. Ted and Emma made their own Sloe Gin from the sloes that grew along the hedgerows of their many acres back in Wales. His father had taught him when he was a boy and they collectively gathered bucketsful every year. He remembered his parents sitting together around the table in the evening pricking each sloe with a silver fork – it had to be silver, his father had stated categorically, otherwise all you would end up with was syrup! It had never failed, and year after year they decanted at least a couple of bottles of the 'good stuff'.

Neither of them had ever been big drinkers but occasionally, for some special reason, or on the rare occasion they had visitors, they would treat themselves to a glass or two and it certainly loosened Emma's inhibitions!

It seemed so many years ago now though, Ted reflected. The arrival of the children for one thing had put paid to having the odd tipple once the sun had gone over the yard arm, they were too exhausted, but in the grand scheme of things, did it matter if one did partake in the odd glass or two? Wasn't life too short to worry about indulgences of any description?

Those poor young sods on the battlefields just a decade ago wouldn't have worried about the affect their livers would suffer through drinking! Not at all, more so the enemy bullets, etcetera! How much easier it would have been to have confronted the enemy and advance into battle having drank themselves into oblivion beforehand. Death would have been less fearful, less painful, perhaps even more easy as their inhibitions had been abandoned. Did the Jacobite's go into battle at Culloden, fuelled on whiskey?

He was happy that he made the decision to come up to Scotland to see Billy fight his first fight. He was glad he'd made peace with Ivan too, concluding that if the worst came to the worst, he'd know that Billy was where he chose to be. He may have been 'dumped' in their barn all those years back but he had followed his heart and was obviously thriving.

"Davy, Emma would like to find a wool shop while we're here in Scotland. She likes to knit and would like to be able to find some quality wools, and I'd like to try some quality whiskey too, so if you can oblige on both accounts, we'd be most grateful."

"Ye should have said, Ted," Davy said smiling again, "it just so happens there's a fine guest house ahead, about five miles if I'm correct. The proprietor's brother is a friend o' Dougal's and he works at Bell's Distilleries, hahaha. Every night after he's finished his shift, he sneaks back to the empty barrels that are left outside and he drains each and every one. Of course, I have nae told ye this! He fills loads of bottles and gives 'em to his brother, which he sells on t' his customers. It's money in both pockets - if ye get ma drift."

"Will they have a telephone at this guest house?" asked Billy, "I'd like to tell Hank about the stuff I've got of Benny Lynch's and I want to know if he's heard any more news about Norman."

The guest house was small, quaint and comfortable, but didn't have a telephone, so Billy would have to wait until he got back to launch into the telling of his news. Ted,

Emma, Billy and Marley shared the 'family room' while Davy had the single. Marley took out her owl and studied it meticulously, gazing into the glass dome at its eyes, the feathers and its overall 'knowing' demeanour. She'd never seen one this close up, before, 'as wise as an owl,' she muttered to herself.

Billy took out the boxing gloves and tried them on for size, they were far too big but felt good on his young hands. He experienced an overwhelming sense of closeness to Benny Lynch, wearing his boxing gloves and he turned to Ted to show him. "Will I grow into them, Dad?" he asked, turning his hands over and over.

"I'll wash those shorts, get the blood out, though I'm sure they'll need a darned good soaking before they come clean," Emma said, picking out the shorts from the box.

"Oh no," cried Billy, "no, that would be washing out Benny Lynch! No, Mum, you cannot wash them. If I ever become a boxer, and good enough to wear his stuff, I'll be proud to have him in the ring with me."

Emma had procured a little knick-knack too. It was a very unusual and very sweet Royal Worcester ornament, about five inches in height. It was half woman, half bird. The female part was wearing a lime-green, long, flowing dress, but the head was that of a bird. Her human hands were holding a song book while the head was tipped backwards in full thrust of a song, the beak wide open. It was a candle snuffer, she knew that just by the shape of it, but also recognised the significance of it being Jenny Lind, the Swedish opera singer renowned as the 'Swedish Nightingale' - one of the most highly regarded singers of the nineteenth century. Emma was enthralled by the little ornament which she anticipated placing on her dressing table and was humbled when Jock Black said he wouldn't take a penny for it.

An off-chance visit to the simple 'junk yard' had had a positive effect on them all and they'd left with memories and memorabilia to last a lifetime. Emma had thanked Jock profusely and gave him a big departing hug, vowing to return again one day.

Chapter 25: A Patch of Yellow

Terry loved coming back to Inverness! It was a relief to escape the harsh, brutal and remote climes of the Shetland Isles, day in day out of rain, grey clouds, and the bitter cold. Warm summer days were few and far between and when the sun did eventually decide to show its face, it was like heaven on earth. The peace, tranquillity and obscurity offered a blanket of anonymity and detachment from the real world. The other crofters despised him though, considered him creepy and tried to avoid him and the whole family.

The Irvings were altogether an odd lot, the locals decided, especially the *male* Irvings - in particular the father, 'Patch' Irving! Nobody could quite understand how the lovely, former nurse of the First World War, had married this foreboding brute of a man.

Charlotte – Lotty to everyone, had been William's nurse after he suffered an eye injury during WW I. Oh, he had been an absolute pussycat then, charming, alluring - the perfect patient and gentleman! Grateful, polite, lovable; who wouldn't have fallen for him? Lotty could not have done. She fell truly, madly, deeply. So much so that, at his behest, she followed him after the war to the other end of her world - the Shetland Isles, a million eons away from her life in South East London, and what a culture shock that had turned out to be! Out in the Shetland Isles with mile after mile of... *nothingness*. No markets to frequent to buy vegetables, no friendly neighbours to interact or chat with, and only one ferry to the mainland every now and again! A culture shock indeed.

But a promise was a promise and she'd given hers to William, the charming patient who had assured her that they would have the perfect life together when all the ugliness of war was over. They would fill their home and their lives with lots of beautiful children and she would encounter a happiness she could never imagine.

Their abode was an extremely primitive, thatched dwelling, as most properties on the island were. A small, rented cottage on a croft with just two rooms downstairs and two up – living quarters and sleeping quarters – the peat stacked up in neat piles against the perimeter fence. It was bleak, draughty and cold most times with the peat supplies for the fireplace being tightly rationed. It had taken Lotty many months to transform their grim surroundings into something at least a little prettier, thanks to her needlework skills. She'd made curtains for the windows and doors from salvaged tweeds and tartans bartered and exchanged between crofters for whatever anyone's needs were negotiable.

Lotty found herself pregnant after only weeks of being in – what was to her – another dimension in the unfamiliar universe. She was, predictably, nervous. Her perfect body was going to grow bigger and the few clothes she had were not going to fit much longer. And whilst this was supposed to bring newlyweds closer together, her husband made her feel like she, alone, had single-handedly committed a crime beyond redemption.

Her William changed from the charming, gallant gent she'd lovingly nursed back to health, into an unrecognisable pig. The happiness he promised she would never imagine, was far too short-lived and she had no idea why.

Lotty was no midwife but she *was* a nurse and knew she was in trouble with her second birth. She'd endured a worrying and miserable pregnancy and when her contractions started shortly after only eight months, she felt something amiss with the positioning of the baby. Her nursing expertise didn't pertain to midwifery but her colleagues did, and when she found herself in the predicament of premature labour she was greatly concerned.

Her uncaring husband was ambivalent to her duress and ignored her pleas for him to reach out to a neighbour to come and help. He took up his fishing rod and left the croft, away from the pitiful crying and moaning of a woman he no longer considered innocent, attractive and therefore worthy of his attentions.

Her baby was not going to be born normally and it was going to be all up to her, alone, to deliver the child into this meaningless and empty world of hers.

She dragged herself over to the little table where her husband kept his cutthroat razor for shaving. It was slightly rusty as he only shaved once in a blue moon - his personal hygiene routine as diminished as their affection towards each other.

She had not the time, inclination, or the means to boil the razor as she writhed and groaned in agony. She held the blade in her right hand and sent silent prayers upwards as she sliced at the bottom of her belly, just above her pubic hairline... and passed out with the pain.

It was young Terry who walked in and found his mother soaked in her own blood, cold, still and silent, her eyes wide open. He had never seen a naked body before and was confused to see a tiny human-being half-submerged from his mother's belly. He could see it moving though no sound came from it. He crouched down in front of his mother's legs, worrying that he would be scolded for getting his knees bloodied, and he reached inside to pick up the baby by its arm, dragging it towards him and wondered why on earth it was attached to something 'rope-like' by its stomach. He couldn't detach it so he picked up the cutthroat razor that was in his mother's hand and severed the umbilical cord and almost dropped the baby there and then when it took its first breath and wailed!

He sat there for the longest time watching it. He didn't know what it was, even. He kept trying to talk to his mother, asking her if she was ok, why was she so cold, why was she on the floor bleeding, and what was he supposed to do? He didn't know where his father was and worried that he would be thrashed for causing a mess that his mother now seemed incapable of cleaning. He considered running off, as far away as he could, but this thing was screaming and even though he was only five years old something told him he should keep it warm because his mother felt very cold. He looked around the tiny room but there was nothing suitable so he put his mother's skirt down, covering her modesty and the crying thing, then he got up and ran outside, and he continued running and running.

Yes, Inverness was a relief. He could forget everything here, all the past trials and tribulations, his tyrannical father, his simpleton of a sister, his non-existent lifestyle and walk amongst unjudgmental people, like an invisible entity.

He had come to buy medical supplies. Simple things mostly like bandages, poultices, creams, lotions and potions. He'd read all of his mother's medical books that she had brought to the Shetlands with her, and he'd learned well, well enough to be confident at treating the locals!

There was no qualified doctor, per se, on the island, so the crofters came to the Irvings for all their medicinal needs. 'Patch' Irving rubbed his thick, grubby hands together every time a potential customer called, charging extortionate rates. It was his idea to branch out further on the mainland to set up an apothecary business, assuring himself that all he had to do was buy and stock the supplies, and the customers would come in their drones.

And the customers did come! He found suitable premises in Buccleuch Street and took on the lease, gleefully leaving his 'needy' family behind on the Shetland Isles and counting the ha'pennies, pennies and pounds every night like Ebenezer Scrooge . . . until he received his call-up. He was furious, convinced he'd previously done 'his bit' when he fought in the First World War and had tried his utmost to wheedle his way out of it, but there was nothing wrong with his eyesight, he was just scarred grotesquely, his eyelid lashes and brow burned away, the patch was purely cosmetic.

His son, however, was far more cunning and astute and inherited the same cowardly attributes as his father, declaring his inability to join his comrades was due to his mental health problems, of which he was able to convince everyone perfectly!

He had been trying to think up a plan to avoid his conscription and cunningly began to plot his escape. He would deliberately wet and foul himself all the time, he never shaved or bathed. He would trap pigeons and rats and tie their dead bodies around his waist and neck as he paraded around for everyone to see. He'd wail and scream obscenities to anyone who came anywhere near him so that the whole community thought he'd completely lost his mind, some blaming a delayed reaction on finding his mother all those years back. Others remained unconvinced.

'Patch' sent a telegram to his son telling him he should come to Edinburgh to keep the business going in his absence. He was no fool, he knew his son, and Terry had kept every single white feather that had been left at his threshold in a little silk purse that had belonged to his mother; some had been painted yellow – the mark of a coward. But Terry didn't care, he found it all very amusing. He glued all the feathers, white and yellow, onto a dead pigeon and hung it over the church door the day he took the ferry and left for Edinburgh to take over his father's apothecary business. He was free!

William 'Patch' Irving didn't want to return to Edinburgh after his second stint of war, he wanted to pack it all in and live out the rest of his days in peace and tranquillity of his homeland, hoping his kin had already fled the nest and he could live alone, comfortably, but he was obligated into going to make the final arrangements.

He had no friends – period. He had no 'war buddies' whatsoever he could meet up with for a pint and talk about their war experiences as hundreds and hundreds often did. He could never rely on another single human and likewise none had ever been able to rely on him! William Irving was always the last man to leave the trenches. He was the one who would shake and cry and wet himself like a 'wee timorous beastie' when ordered to go over the top. He was the one who would stagger and fall, feigning dead while the real brave men fought to defend their colleagues and countries. William Irving was a pathetic excuse for a *man* and unfortunately his son took after him rather than his brave and wonderful mother . .

He could definitely not be relied on for support in any shape or form, which he proved on many occasions – earning the well-deserved nickname down the trenches, of 'Patch Yellow'.

He truly felt that he had left that stigma behind him when Lotty became his wife, and they began life anew in his sanctuary away from the gossip and memories. Until his second calling, of course, when he had been reminded that mud sticks, and embarrassingly found himself once again alongside the formidable Douglas Reddick, and his heart sank.

Douglas Reddick did not suffer fools gladly, neither did he suffer cowards, and it was he who came up with the perfect descriptive name Patch Yellow, even *before* he wore an eye patch! It was going to be 'Yellow Streak', or 'Yelly Belly'. Oh, he had a handful of phrases and delighted in bantering it about to garner support from the other men in the trenches, those courageous, valiant men, *real* guys who would watch your back, cover you, look out for you - those nothing at all like William Irving! Yes, 'Patch Yellow' perfectly described that streak of cowardice.

His frustration and humiliation being further compounded by the fact that he found himself sleeping, eating and praying alongside some of the people he would give his right arm not to be! The bloody Ralston boys who owned the very gym next door to his apothecary, Hank, Davy and Dougal. How Ivan wished he'd joined the ruddy Navy!

He wasn't altogether alone though in the torment he received, and he relished taking a backseat and watched how the others turned to ridicule the Welshman among them; some Nancy-dancing boy who liked to entertain those in the trenches. He had to admit he was very entertaining with his humorous and theatrical renditions; everybody clapped, sang and joined along with him every single night! Didn't matter what had gone off earlier, the wounded being dragged back down into the trenches, the horrific squeals of the horses as they were blown to smithereens, the blood curdling cries of men and boys as they lay dying, bloodied, wounded; the Welshman reminded them that they were still alive and encouraged them to live for another day.

The soldiers clapped as the young vivacious Ivan entertained the troops. His daily lashings of verbal abuse - and a lot of physical - he took as his due, until the day that Davy stepped up to join in and offer moral support. Nobody knew that Davy and Ivan were already 'acquainted', Hank and Dougal certainly didn't and when everyone watched their rendition of 'Kiltie birdie had a pig, it could do the Irish jig. . " the older brothers watched in silence. Hank sought out Dougal with a confused glare, feeling the Ralstons were being ridiculed, and he was the only one not amused!

Terry was livid - he wanted to continue living in Edinburgh where he felt needed and free. He hated having to go back to the Shetlands at his father's behest to ensure all was 'tickety boo' at the croft, but at least he was able to catch up with Lillian!

He hated her, truth be known, but he loved her too.

What is that dividing line between love and hate? Two immensely powerful words, but both drew him towards Lillian. He hated her, yet he had loved her. He had caressed her face and body told her that she was 'as pretty as a picture' and she had smiled at him, innocently trusting him, and allowed him to violate her and take away her virginity. Her father would kill him with his bare hands if ever he was to find out, and her too! Thankfully, he was away at war, killing men and fighting for his country. He would never know!

It started to drizzle as Ted, Emma, Davy and the two children were walking around one of the little cobbled streets in Inverness. It was steeped in history and the buildings were fascinating. They ran for shelter and found themselves in front of the pillar-fronted former school in Margaret Street - now a courthouse / police-station / theatre - waiting for the rain to subside. Someone else also ran for shelter and distanced himself from them, took out a packet of cigarettes from his jacket pocket and lit up, a cloud of smoke rising into the damp air.

Billy couldn't take his eyes off the man and felt an uncomfortable churning in the pit of his stomach.

"Billy, don't stare, it's rude to stare" Emma told him. He had no conception why, but he felt afeared of the tall, greasy-haired man sheltering at the other end of the entrance.

Then the rain stopped as quickly as it had appeared and everyone laughed as they walked away, in an endeavour to locate the wool shop Emma wanted to find. Well, everyone laughed except Billy.

Chapter 26: Growing Up

Billy had had his sixteenth birthday and Marley her twelfth. Emma was now a widow and Trefellon was no longer a sheep farm. Ted had passed away nine months after the trip to Edinburgh they'd made to see Billy's debut boxing match against Jimmy Watts, and it was a trip that he had been thankful he made.

The 1960s was turning out to be the most liberating era ever. Music was changing. Bands of men formed into groups such as The Beatles or The Rolling Stones, pumping out loud, intoxicating songs, inciting young girl-fans into a libidinous frenzy. Fashions were changing, too, with men shying away from the buttoned-down, neck-tied, starched shirts in favour of more casual attire, while women were dressing in ways that showed off their feminine attributes.

Technology was speeding ahead, too, with few homes not having the luxury of a telephone. Many people were acquiring more and more modern, time-saving household goods – sometimes 'on tick' or the 'never-never' – televisions and washing machines. Cinemas were filled to capacity with eager punters excited to see the newest films displayed on huge screens. Roads were becoming more heavily populated with colourful, streamlined cars. Conscription was finally over. What a time to be alive!

Ivan had not been surprised at the sudden decline in Ted's health and eventual passing as he had spoken at great length with him during their tête-à-tête. He'd confided to Ivan that he had Leukaemia, an aggressive form – Acute Myeloid Leukaemia, the most common in men of his age - and spoke of his plans to sell off his livestock so that Emma and Marley wouldn't have the burden of maintaining the sheep farm. He had asked Ivan to ensure the two siblings kept in touch as often as possible and begged him to continue looking after Billy as if he was his own flesh and blood, and Ivan reassured him that he would. Of course he would, and he and Billy took the train to Aberdovey, on that devastating Tuesday afternoon after receiving the telephone call, to support Emma and Marley and pay their final respects.

It perplexed Billy to be back in Wales for his father's funeral, he had seemed non-perturbed, confused and a *little* sad but that was about all. He knew he should feel gratitude to the two people he referred to as 'mum and dad' but felt little more and couldn't wait to return to Edinburgh.

The years had distanced him from his sister too and the phone calls and letters had filtered to the obligatory birthdays and Christmases.

He still attended his school and maintained his dancing and his boxing.

Norman no longer frequented the gym, his hearing - allegedly - never fully regained, besides which Anne, his mother, withdrew her support, blaming Hank for their trauma. Billy learned that Norman had packed his bags one day and left to seek his fortune in London where he believed the streets were paved with gold and though Anne checked her mailbox daily, anticipating a letter from him, not one was ever received.

Ivan's dream, however, was turning out to be a massive success story and it was fully underway. 'Star Struck' was blooming and night after night after night tens of scores of punters flooded through the doors. Queues of partygoers and revellers from all over came to his venue to be

243

entertained, and they all left with a yen and a promise to return.

He'd deliberated over names for his establishment and changed his mind a hundred times until the very day the signage guys had arrived and just casually announced that it was going to be 'Star Struck'. He had no notion where the name came from but stood fast and the sign was up in less than three hours.

It was a very daring, avant-garde enterprise but Ivan felt there was an audience for such a place and every single member of his staff was interviewed by him, and Davy.

The construction company had been excellent. They listened to his demands and ideas and the whole place oozed 'class' and extravaganza! The stage boasted festooned drapes and overhead lighting with spotlights in all corners. A compere box and microphone for announcing the various acts had been erected at the far end of the stage. The bar was filled with optics for spirits, liqueurs, wines, and beer-barrel pumps. Underneath counters housed hundreds of glasses, cocktail sticks, jars of cherries and sliced lemons, packets of peanuts and crisps.

There was an entrance fee of sixpence per person, payable at the kiosk at the front door, and Ivan had insisted on this to keep away the riff-raff, the drunks and probable troublemakers.

All his staff were male and Ivan had made it abundantly clear that Star Struck was a sanctuary for them all to be who they wanted to be. If they wanted to don braces or blusher and bras, it was up to them.

The dancers would come every afternoon to practise their cabaret renditions and can-can dancing, dressed in frills and feathers, tuxedos and tutus.

Billy loved Star Struck! He loved the people who came every day to practise the shows they were going to produce to the punters, later. He loved to watch them dress in their finery and dance to the modern music blasting out from the speakers in each corner of the stage. They all flirted and teased him, provoking him into joining them in their various outlandish and flamboyant acts but Billy was biding his time. He had his very own act up his sleeve!

He had also become aware of a different kind of relationship between Ivan and Davy. He knew they had always been 'close' and remembered vague snippets about them being together during the war, or before; but as he was maturing himself, he found he was becoming somewhat *envious* of their friendship! They laughed with each other a little longer than necessary and their eyes seemed to twinkle more than if Ivan was talking to anyone else. He'd never known Ivan to have a girlfriend or even talk about wanting one, and that fact didn't altogether surprise him because, indeed, he was just as non-committal in that department.

It began to dawn on Billy that perhaps Ivan and Davy were much the same as he, and if there was ever a good and supportive person to talk about such things as his insecurities, maybe it was the man who he regarded as a paternal figure, the one he had opted to call 'Pops'.

It was a usual, normal Thursday morning, no different to all the others come and gone over the years, when Ivan entered Billy's bedroom, minus his prosthetic leg, waving a newspaper in his hand.

"Bill. Billy, wake up, you need to see this."

The front cover was showing Star Struck. Ivan was buzzing with excitement, "Billy, look what they're saying about us. It's fantastic coverage. Look here, there's a picture of me, and see here, the guys on the stage! It says 'come and be prepared to be struck dumb at Star Struck'! Ha, what d'you think, hey? Read it Bill. This is going to draw 'em in."

Billy forced himself to sit upright, trying to focus on the newspaper thrust in front of his sleepy eyes. He looked at the headlines and at Ivan's euphoric, anticipated expression, and began to read... "Only the brave dare to tread where others have feared and the young Welshman, Ivan Rhys, has done just that, bringing a new dimension of entertainment to our city. It is here at *Star Struck* where one can enjoy the spectacular performance of a new dimension, in the theatre of the future..."

"I think you've done it, Pops. Have Hank and the others seen this?" he looked beseechingly at Ivan, "this is going to be good for the gym, too."

"I don't know. Davy just gave it to me, so I presume so."

It was just after seven am. "Davy has been here already?" asked Billy.

"You know Davy! People to see, places to go," and he left Billy to ponder the newspaper story . . and the reason why Davy had already been in their apartment at seven a.m. in the morning!

The phone was ringing in the hallway of Star Struck and Ivan answered, expecting it to be a supplier of wines or beers, and was delighted to hear the soft feminine but knowing and affirmative voice he recognised as his very own adorable Marley. "Hello Uncle Ivan, is Billy there, please?"

"Of course he is, Princess, hang on, I'll get him . . . BILLY" he shouted upstairs, "hang on Marls, . . BILLLLLYYYY!"

Billy thundered down the stone staircase wearing only his y-fronts and grabbed the receiver from Ivan. "What? have I forgotten your birthday?".

Marley chuckled at the other end of the line, "not mine Billy, but it looks like you forgot mum's as there was no card from you yesterday. Will it arrive today?"

Billy was horrified! "Is she up already?"

"No, she's still asleep. I'm off to school now so you can call her later to wish her a happy birthday."

The phone went dead and Billy held the receiver out, listening to the beeps as he frantically tried to think of something he could do to redeem himself.

He waited until just before nine o'clock when he should have been in class, but he would rather face the wrath of his teacher for being late than the disappointment of his mother for forgetting her birthday!

"Lavender blue, dilly-dilly, lavender green. When I am king, dilly-dilly, you'll be my queen . . " he sang into the mouthpiece. "Hey Mum, happy birthday. Did you get my card?" he lied.

He knew his mum held this song dear to her heart and he never forgot the first time she sang it with him.

She didn't answer his question, instead . . . "who told me so? Dilly-dilly, who told me so? I told myself, Billy-Billy, I told me so," she laughed at the other end of the telephone, "yes, I received your lovely card this morning. Thank you," she lied.

Billy ended the call and walked out onto the streets of Edinburgh to his school. He studied the people he encountered and wondered if everybody lied about things the way he had just done with his mother, and she with him, and for what purpose?

A 'white lie' perhaps to pacify his mum so that she wouldn't feel disappointed that he'd not given her a second thought but that wasn't entirely true, he did think about his family down there in Wales even though he felt a huge distance, now. He wasn't even sure he had any true brotherly feelings towards Marley, his own sister. They were so different, in looks, personalities, lifestyles and ambitions. He felt close to her but in a detached way, almost in an obligatory way.

He decided to skip school that day and walked around Edinburgh city centre, around the castle grounds and the flower clock, justifying his truancy knowing he would be leaving imminently to find employment. He walked to the Grassmarket and patted Greyfriars Bobby on his head, the bronze gleaming from hundreds of other hands doing the same. Three youths gathered on the street corner smoking cigarettes watched him smiling at a statue of a little dog and decided to have some fun. "Hey Nancy," one bravely shouted over to Billy, "looks like the only puppies you've had your hands on is our Bobby there." His sidekicks chuckled: Billy ignored them and carried on walking.

"Hey, don't walk away, we just wanna get to know you." They threw down their cigarettes, walking towards him. They circled him, smiling, and Billy knew they were looking for trouble.

"I don't want to get to know you though, so if you let me pass, no one will get hurt."

The three roared even louder. "Hurt? Och ginger, I don't think *you* could hurt a fly," said the first one, the other two closing in.

Billy instinctively ducked down, then head butted the ringleader in the stomach who doubled over in pain, falling to his knees, the two others moved back an inch or two in surprise.

"I wouldn't know where to hit you other two to save your lives, so like I said earlier, let me pass and no one else will get hurt."

The long-haired youth lunged at Billy and they toppled over, landing on top of each other. 'Ringleader', holding his stomach, shouted to his buddy to 'show him what a real man does to a disrespectful Nancy-boy'. He was about to throw a punch when Billy grabbed his wrist and followed with a blow to his chin causing his head to fall back. He then managed to heave himself up, throwing 'long-hair' off to the side, and he leapt up onto his feet.

"If that's the best you can do, looks like I'm not the Nancy-boy here after all."

'Ringleader' was impressed and started to laugh. "Round one to you Nancy. Hey, looks like we were mistaken, no hard feelings pal. Shall we shake hands, kiss and make up? What d'ya say?"

Billy thought quickly, "I say you guys need a bit more practise. Meet me at Hank's gym tonight, seven o'clock, see who the *real* man is then . . . hey?" He brushed himself up and walked away, leaving the three clowns feeling very miffed.

Sure enough at seven o'clock the very three youths sauntered into Hank's gym. Billy knew they would, he was already dressed in his shorts, vest, boots and gloves, anticipating their arrival. He'd forewarned Dougal about their earlier altercation and made him promise not to breathe a word about his truancy! Ivan would not be pleased.

The three cocky young men, Mike (ringleader), Joe (long-hair), and Guy (no.3) all local, looked around the place in awe! They'd heard about Hank's gym – everyone had, but never dreamt of stepping foot inside, considering their fighting skills adequate enough for the streets, their 'hood'.

They spotted Billy in the ring, sporting a headguard, pursuing Dougal with his bag gloves up in front of his face, pounding away at a frightening force and speed. "Your new pals have arrived," he whispered and Billy stopped, turning to look at his humbled audience.

He climbed out of the ring taking off his headguard and offered it to Mike. "This is where I prove myself, here – in the ring. Take your shoes off, put this on and some gloves and I'll repay *you* a lesson."

253

"A lesson?" Mike asked.

"You taught me a valuable lesson today. A reason why it is not a good idea to skip school and hang around on street corners, like a loser. You showed me the importance of having an education."

Mike was furious, how dare the Nancy-boy belittle him so, and in front of everyone! He kicked off his shoes, threw his jacket onto the floor and quickly put on a pair of gloves as he climbed into the ring. Dougal sat below with the two others, gleefully anticipating a blood bath.

It was an exceedingly entertaining performance indeed. Billy put his heart and soul into ridiculing his older opponent, dancing around him on his tip toes, shuffling backwards and sidewards to avoid an outlandish punch from the pathetic novice who had no clue about protecting his face or body against stylish and professional attacks. The smoker who was struggling to keep up with the fitness and determination of the one who aimed to be the next Benny Lynch, mocking his every move. He was defeated, he knew, and now had a decision to make – to acknowledge defeat to the younger man or stand his ground and carry on the war.

His buddies made his decision for him as they rose from their seats alongside Dougal, cheering for Billy. For Mike, it was a bitter pill to swallow but he also had to admit that that afternoon had proved to be a turning point in his life. He had considered Billy as an easy pushover, totally underestimating his opponent, and he was right, they had both learned a very valuable lesson that day.

Billy changed from his boxing attire into his normal clothes and approached the trio as he was leaving, "thank you for coming, all of you, but I have to go now, gotta help my Pops next door – he's got a big night tonight and as much as I'd like to hang around on street corners with you guys, I'm afraid I have to earn my keep."

The three stared at him, "Star Struck is YOURS?" asked Joe in amazement, "my Gran never stops talking about your dad!"

Billy didn't feel the need to correct him, adding "you can come in, if you want to, but don't even think of asking for a free drink."

They followed him next door into Star Struck like they had just won a huge amount of money on Littlewoods Pools, walking past the ticket kiosk without having to pay a single penny and could not wait to get home that night to tell their respective families everything they had encountered.

Guy lay in his bed and reached for a book on his bedside cabinet. He looked at the cover page and tossed it aside, thinking how boring it was bound to be. And then he reconsidered, 'don't judge a book by its cover' . . . he picked it up and began reading the first few pages, the next several chapters, and it was two in the morning when he switched off his lamp and fell fast asleep.

Chapter 27: Who am I?

Billy was approaching the end of his school days and needed a National Insurance Number to enable him to secure a job. In his heart-of-hearts he knew only one avenue he wanted to pursue - boxing! He had spent many years dreaming of following in Benny Lynch's footsteps and becoming the next boxer to represent Scotland. He trained every single weeknight in the gym and on Saturdays he ran from Buccleuch Street to the train station and back. He did push-ups, press-ups and pull-ups. He and Guy spent every Sunday morning running backwards and racing competitively from the flower clock on Princes Street to the gym on Buccleuch Street, panting, laughing and sweating profusely. Guy had quit smoking now, as had Mike and Joe, earnestly trying to get fit so that they too could be regarded as 'proper boxers'.

Billy was a good, upcoming amateur boxer and had enjoyed polishing his collection of trophies that adorned the shelf in his bedroom, seven now and counting. He would love to become professional like Terry Downs and Sugar Ray Robinson who he read about in all the boxing magazines, but he knew he needed more accolades under his belt for any decent manager to take him onboard. He would have liked at least an ABA title, but he was too impatient. Dougal and Hank kept him grounded, reminding him that he was still young.

Ivan wanted him to help out at Star Struck, take on a more managerial part, ordering stock, bookkeeping, banking, etc., knowing he was more than capable of doing it all and Ivan needed someone he could trust, a right-hand man. He told Billy to get down to the careers office and obtain a National Insurance number so that he could pay him, or get a job elsewhere, but anyway, he would need a number.

There were two other people in the office besides Billy; one girl he knew from school and the other boy he didn't know. Both were being attended to by the careers advisors and both had left smiling, having accomplished what they had come for.

There was a lady advisor of roughly forty years old who reminded Billy of a former teacher in Aberdovey, one that he was a little daunted by. She wore thick, winged spectacles and her auburn hair was tied severely back from her face. The younger male advisor seemed more approachable, and he hoped that he would be attended to by him. He was not in luck though, as he was called to the desk of his former look-alike teacher who gestured to him to sit down.

"How can I help you?" she asked expressionlessly, "are you looking for a job?"

"No, not really. I was advised to come here to get a National Insurance number," he replied.

"Birth certificate please," she asked.

He hadn't considered this, and evidently neither had Ivan. "Oh, I didn't know I needed it."

"Have you already secured employment?"

"In a way . . I suppose."

She put down her pen and stared at Billy. "In a way?"

"My Pops wants me to learn the ropes at the bar, you know – bookkeeping, stocktaking, etc, perhaps working behind the bar too at busy times."

"Hmm, a barman, then?"

"No, not really a barman, but in way I suppose sometimes I would be classed as that, yes. But sometimes I might be needed to help out with the acts, singing, dancing and stuff."

He had her full attention now and she removed her glasses, her smile spreading from ear to ear. Everyone had heard about the new bar and she wanted to know as much as she could, deciding she might even wangle a courtesy pass if she looked after the 'son' of the owner, who was quite a celebratory by all accounts!

"I'm Gail Preston," she announced, leaning over to shake Billy's hand, "I've heard lots of fabulous reports about Star Struck and I'm dying to see it for myself. Oh, how wonderful it must be to be part of such a unique enterprise! Tell me, is it true that all the dancers are really men dressed as women, they wear make-up and beautiful clothes? And the bar staff too, they're all men?"

"Hmm," he nodded, "but not everyone is dressed as a woman. The comedians, the lighting and sound guys don't. My Pops doesn't and I definitely don't!"

She sat waiting for him to continue, fascinated to hear more.

"This National Insurance number then, I have to bring a birth certificate. Why, what for, why can't you just give me a number?"

"It's necessary; we need your date of birth and where you were born. Just bring your birth certificate in whenever you're able and we will issue you with your own National Insurance number. Bring it to *me* because I will remember you."

Billy stood up and left the office, worried about what he was going to tell Ivan. He'd never seen his birth certificate and he knew that that rogue August Mensah hadn't fulfilled his obligation into making their adoption legal! Where was this going to leave him?

He went back home and found Ivan stocking up the bar with spirits, and the sound guy was fiddling about with the acoustics and sound checking. A comedian from London was performing tonight and he was bringing a coachload of fans along. It was going to be another busy night.

"Ivan," Billy said quietly, "the bint at the careers office said I need to show her my birth certificate, without it she can't issue me a number."

Ivan's face registered the realisation. Naturally he would need to produce this document, it just hadn't crossed his mind! "Shit Bill, I'm sorry, I didn't think. Crikey, what are we going to do? You don't have one — thanks to that bloody scoundrel Mensah." He covered his mouth with his hands, looking at Billy standing in front of him waiting for him to make everything all right, as he always did.

And then he just laughed out loud. "Well, a bit long overdue but guess it's about time we did something about it, don't you think? Come on, let's go back and see the 'bint' and find out what our options are."

Gail Preston's face lit up when she saw Billy and Ivan walk through the doors, gesturing for them both to come over and take a seat in front of her, removing her glasses in the hope of making her look more attractive, Ivan was single, after all! "Billy, nice to see you again so soon and you've brought your father with you I take it?"

Billy turned to Ivan hoping he was going to take over the dealings.

"Miss Preston," Ivan addressed, "we have a little problem, are you terribly busy right now?"

Ivan spent the next half hour informing 'Miss Preston' of Billy's circumstances. "So you see, the Talberts assumed they had adopted Billy and his sister legally, but we now have reason to believe that the idiot lawyer didn't do what he had promised and drank away the money he had been paid. Billy is sixteen years old Miss Preston, as far as we know. We cannot be sure of his precise date of birth or where he was born, though we have always had an inkling they came from somewhere in Scotland and that assumption is based purely on Billy's accent as a child."

Gail Preston sat and listened throughout; she'd never heard of such a sad and woeful tale. Billy and Ivan watched her digest the information, waiting for her to say something encouraging.

"Mr Rhys, Billy. I don't honestly know where this is all going to lead. It's… well, it's all very very unusual, I can't promise to find your parents, Billy," she said turning to

Billy, "but I do know an excellent lawyer here who I could put you in touch with to make you, Ivan, his legal guardian."

Ivan and Billy smiled at each other. "That would be perfect. Here's our telephone number, Edinburgh 216. We'll wait to hear from you?"

They would indeed hear from her, the minute they left she was on the telephone to her brother, Barry - the best lawyer in Edinburgh!

Barry Preston was like a breath of fresh air and instantly Ivan and Billy felt confident that he was going to do everything he positively assured them he would do. They'd been in his company for less than forty minutes but felt they had known him for a lifetime! He'd never heard of August Mensah though he claimed he knew many of the same ilk.

"I have to say Billy, that you are indeed a very fortunate young man having so many people love you and attempting to become your legal guardians. Any woman can become a mother, as indeed any man can be a father, but only an exceptional person can be a Mum or Dad, do you understand what I'm saying?" Billy nodded, turning to grin at Ivan, the one he'd chosen to be his Pops.

"My two boys didn't have the choice you have, they got lumbered with me and my Missus, I'm afraid," he chuckled.

"So, I'm to understand, Mr Rhys, that it's your wish to become Billy's legal guardian, am I right?"

Ivan nodded, "I believe so, but is there a chance I can legally adopt him, as my own, I mean?"

"There has been zero parental contact throughout their entire lives. No letters, no 'phone calls, no visits . . .?"

"None, nothing," Ivan interrupted.

"And Billy, I understand that you left your . . the people you considered to be your parents, to follow Mr Rhys, is that correct? You wanted to be with him? Could you tell me why, were they cruel to you, did you not like them?"

Billy looked mortified. "No, not at all. They are lovely people, I called them Mum and Dad and my sister is very happy living there. I just felt closer to Ivan, that's all. I didn't want him to leave. I love my life here, in Edinburgh."

"Ok, that's good, I understand. Well, who wouldn't love Edinburgh, hey? We Scots are exceedingly proud of our magnificent country. I believe you do a bit of boxing too, Billy? Tell me, who do you aspire to?"

Without any hesitation he replied, "Benny Lynch. I have his gear and one day I'm gonna wear it and win. Make him proud."

"Well, I hope you don't end up like our Benny Lynch," he chuckled, "fine, fine boxer, but he succumbed to the drink, as I'm sure you know if you're an ardent fan of his, but what about these American boxers, hey? Do you ever see yourself in the ring against one of those? The Yanks have always done better and bigger than most."

"We will have to wait and see, Mr Preston, sir, but I think your money is safe on me. I'm grounded, disciplined and I train every day. I have the support of my Pops here, and Hank and Dougal from the gym, as well as the love from my mum and my sister. So yes, I think I can give the Yanks a run for their dollars. I also think it might be a huge feather in your cap by giving me an identity; to making my way clear to becoming somebody. Me! For the last sixteen years I've not known who I am. I've always known my name was Billy and my sister is Marley, but that's it. At least your sons are lucky to know who they are, Mr Preston, and who their mum is and where they're from."

Billy continued, "My earliest memories are being in darkness all the time, of feeling lonely and isolated. Pushed into an abyss of fear, hidden out of sight for a reason I had no comprehension of... Marley and me... Well, it was just me until Marley came along – I think? I can't really say. I do have a faint recollection of my mother..." He frowned as he reflected, "I just think 'yellow' and I know that yellow should conjure a happy feeling, like the sun. The sun is supposed to represent warmth and happiness, but I don't feel that. Yellow always makes me feel sad."

"A father figure? Do you remember your father at all?" Barry asked.

Billy smiled at Ivan, then. "My dad, Ted, definitely. He taught me so much and he made the best porridge, ever. I can kinda recall him showing me around the farm, vaguely.

Introducing me to all the animals and Boo, our Border Collie – well... *their* Border Colllie, always having to be with us. I knew, even then, that I liked dogs. I think perhaps I used to have one? Bonnie... I don't know what happened to her." After a pensive pause, Billy finished his thoughts, "But then I guess I got lucky. I got *two* dads, but Ivan is my real dad."

"So," said Barry Preston addressing Ivan, "we're going for adoption?"

"YES", they said in unison!

Two weeks later the phone was ringing in Star Struck and no-one appeared to answer it. It stopped, then rang again. And again.

Chapter 28: Decisions

Ivan could not decide who disliked coming back to Aberdovey the most, he or Billy. They both had valid reasons for their trepidation, albeit both different - or were they? Ivan felt that Billy should have been a lot more supportive to his family than he had been. Marley was just a young girl, and it was natural that she would need her only brother to come home.

Marley found Emma lying unresponsive when she had come home from school, finding her on the kitchen floor with a big gash under her eye, the blood already coagulated. She was absolutely frantic, not having the slightest clue what to do - pacing about, then falling on her knees to cradle her mother - talking to her, beseeching her to tell her what to do next, but Emma didn't, couldn't.

Billy and Ivan were the first people she thought of to call and when she couldn't reach them, she called for assistance.

Now slightly disorientated in a hospital bed, Emma propped herself up with the pillows while her family gathered around, waiting to hear her version of what had happened.

"It was very odd," she began, "the postman had just delivered a letter and as I waved him goodbye, another vehicle drove up. I didn't recognise it, nor the people inside." She looked at the concerned faces around her, anticipating her next words.

"A man got out and he looked very official in his navy-blue suit, and I could also see a young woman sitting in the passenger seat. He was smiling at me so naturally I greeted him, inviting them both to come in, but the woman wouldn't leave, she just sat there." Nobody interrupted her.

"He asked me where the 'bairns' were. I didn't know what he meant so I asked, 'what do you mean, the bairns?'"

"He wanted to know where Billy and Marley were, you mean?" Ivan prompted. Emma nodded.

Billy leapt up from his seat, "what!? Nooo! No, Mum, they can't come here, they can't come back after all this time. They can't take us. Ivan . . ," he implored, "don't let them take us. I'm not going and they're not taking Marley away either."

"Nobody will take either of you, Billy. You have your life in Scotland and Marley's going to stay with your mum. Emma, I have the wheels already in motion to make Billy's adoption legal. I've told him he can either keep your name or use mine, or he can be Billy Rhys-Talbert, but the choice is his. Likewise, I can get the solicitor we're using to do the same adoption procedure for you and Marley, but if someone is trying to reclaim them now, after all these years, we need to act pretty quickly. We don't even know if the children were ever registered, which is something our solicitor is trying to ascertain but he did say that he didn't think they stood any chance as he would fight against them on the grounds of abandonment, neglect, and desertion."

"I never saw the stars or trees until I came to live in Wales, Mum. All I can remember was being in darkness every day, and the fear when the man came. I didn't know what a proper bed was, nice food and having a warm bath and someone to wash me. I only know you and Dad and Ivan as being nice people, who talked to me and looked after us. I will kill whoever it is that is trying to take us away."

"Emma," Ivan said to Emma, dismissing Billy's tirade, "have you considered selling Trefellon and moving?"

She nodded. "My sister, Jennifer, has written to me inviting us to go to America and stay with her for a few months. Yes, I have considered it, Ivan. I would like us to go to America but I'm a little concerned about taking Marley out of school. My sister says America is a grand country, full of wonderful opportunities and the weather is much better there too. But, oh... I don't know..."

Marley stood there with her mouth wide open, "America! to see Auntie Jenny? Mum, of course we should go!"

Billy silently listened to the excitement in his sister's voice, envisaging a brand-new experience before her. His feelings had gone through a whole tumultuous cycle within the past twenty-four hours which left him unable to decide how he actually felt now hearing this new acclamation. His mother hadn't included *him* in the American equation, and he felt that America could be the very place for *him* to become 'somebody' within the boxing fraternity. He could join the ranks of Joe Louis and Sugar Ray Robinson fighting at Caesars Palace and have *his* face pictured in the boxing magazines he bought every month.

Perhaps if he hadn't followed Ivan to Scotland he would be included too, but he loved Ivan and Scotland, and up until these last few minutes listening to his mum's words, never had a single regret. Now he had though; now he *was* having second thoughts. He was having second thoughts about the adoption business too!

"Emma," Ivan went back to why she was here in hospital, "what happened next, after the man asked you where the bairns were?"

"I told him I didn't understand what he was asking, I didn't know what 'bairns' are so I asked him again 'what was he after' and he said he'd come to take them back, and I then realised what he meant, and I panicked. I told him they weren't here. I told him they should leave before I call the police and then the woman got out of the vehicle. She was very young, and I knew - Ivan, I knew it was their mother, it was obvious because she was so like Marley," Emma lowered her head, "he didn't believe the children weren't at home so he pushed by me and went inside to see for himself. Obviously then he knew that I was telling the truth and that's when he hit me, and here I am!"

Billy sat seething, vowing to kill him - whoever it was. He would need his new pals for reinforcement, Guy, Mike, Joe, and the whole of Edinburgh if need be.

He wondered if these people were still here, in Aberdovey, and if indeed it was their mother who had returned to reclaim them. He had always wondered who she was, why she had abandoned them and what she was like, his memories too vague to recall her, but not 'the man', he never forgot the feeling of dread when he was around.

Marley had never shown the slightest interest in her parentage, declaring Ted and Emma her only mum and dad, but not Billy – he had harboured many unanswered questions.

That night, after leaving Emma at the hospital and returning to Trefellon, Billy had decided to call his friends, knowing they'd be at Hank's gym, but Guy wasn't there, it was just Mike and Joe, and Mike was quite taken aback at hearing the hatred spewing out of Billy's mouth about his mum and dad when he'd always spoken so passionately about them. All the lads were. Billy had always hero-worshipped him, and they all agreed they had an enviable relationship, not one of *their* dads had been as supportive as Billy's old man.

Mike reassured him that whatever it took, they would sort it. "That's what friends do for each other, Bill, consider it done. What a bastard! Are you sure about your mum, though?" he asked.

Billy thought about that. Yes, he wanted 'the man' hurt and dead, if he was the dad, but he left all of that for his friends to sort out, his mind wasn't thinking straight, but then... his mother. He hated her yet loved her. That old story adage, love versus hate. He felt he should hate her and yet...

"Enough now, I'm done."

Emma came out of hospital a day or two later, none too untoward after her ordeal but Trefellon had been put on the market for sale, she had decided that once the

275

adoption had been successfully concluded she and Marley would be bound for America, comfortable in the knowledge that Billy was going to be just fine with Ivan.

Ivan returned to Edinburgh alone, leaving Billy to spend his last few weeks with his mother and his sister while they were still here in Wales, before the sale of Trefellon was finalised and they sailed off to begin their new lives in America. He would re-join Ivan in Scotland afterwards.

Truth be told, Billy felt saddened at the prospect of being left behind; that's how he felt about the whole situation. It was easy, or easier, being just at the end of the telephone, or a train journey away, but envisioning them in another country, miles and miles away, troubled him, and for the first time in his young life he acknowledged that blood was thicker than water. Telephone calls to and from America would be expensive and even though that was all the contact he and Marley had from week to week, this was going to be different because *she* was leaving *him*, they both were.

He kept repeating the word 'America' over and over in his head and had to endure the constant excitement and enthusiasm from Marley and his mum as he listened to their non-stop plans for their future.

Marley's ambivalence to Billy's withdrawal hadn't gone unnoticed by Emma but the siblings' estrangement had resulted in this and she concluded that Billy had only himself to chastise. Marley was bubbling over, steadfast in her dreams to go to college and fulfil her life's ambition to become a vet. She was going to have her own practice, her own ranch where she would raise sheep and dogs and horses, and possibly build a Goddam Ark!

They had also procured their necessary passports since Barry Preston had been as good as his sister had promised and actually managed to legalise both adoptions. At long last: Marley was now legally Marley Talbert, adopted daughter of Emma, and Billy was Billy Rhys-Talbert, adopted son of Ivan. Emma had organised that Billy, too, have his own passport, insisting that he visit as soon as they were settled.

He didn't want to leave Wales but at the same time he didn't relish the idea of returning to Edinburgh. He was worried about the people who had come to Trefellon to hurt Emma, and their reasons for being there. Were they he and Marley's parents come to reclaim them? He didn't know; and as intrigued as he was, he didn't want to hang around to find out.

Gail Preston's brother, Barry, was like a strutting peacock at a zoo, delighted to be on the special guest list for Saturday night at Star Struck. He, his wife, and sister, sat in the most prestigious seats front of stage, a complimentary bottle of Champagne cooling in a bucket of ice cubes on their honoured table. Gail constantly looked all around her, hoping everyone would acknowledge that they were guests of honour.

Saturday nights were always extra special. It was the night when everybody dressed to kill and thrill, and that included the entertainers. No expense was spared either by the punters or the proprietor for his preferred guests. In Star Struck, nobody could call out a Scotsman for being 'mean', on the contrary, the pounds flowed as freely as the wines and whiskey! The bar staff were rushed off their feet but never failed to smile at the next person waiting to be served.

The 'girls' were backstage getting their make-up and dresses on, padding out their bras and tucking their tell-tale masculinity inside tights that enhanced their long legs that the women in the audience declared they would die for!

'Lesley Presley' the compere, wore bejewelled dresses befitting royalty, shimmering golds, blues, and silvers, headdresses festooned with plumes of ostrich feathers and necklaces that resembled enormous diamonds, as 'she' announced each act and her repartee never failed to render the audience in stitches. Flamboyant and theatrical personified, the act impressed and entertained, whomever the clientele.

And so, this was the night that Mike Healey had decided to fulfil his obligation to his friend, the one he considered he owed a favour to, having made him realise the need to become a 'man', rather than the street-corner nobody he had always been!

Chapter 29: The Bitter Truth

Billy managed to remain aloof at the train station, fighting back his anxiety and tears after saying goodbye to his sister and his mum. How much easier it was to stand in front of another man with adrenalin flooding through his veins and fight until the bell rang out and be able to blithely walk away. If only life was the same, Billy thought. For somebody else to make those all-important decisions on your behalf and for you not to have need for the slightest concern. Emma, Ted, and Ivan had done that over the years and now, as he sat on the train taking him back to Edinburgh, he understood how privileged he was.

He hadn't been conscripted to fight a war he didn't understand, or been expected to kill another human being just because you were ordered to, like Ivan and the millions of others. *He* had people on his side, in his corner, loving him, nurturing and encouraging him to be whoever he decided to be.

As the train slowly chugged into Edinburgh station, Billy could smell smoke in the air. He grinned to himself remembering the many times he walked up and down the platform at the station and smelled that familiar smell of coming home.

He was still a little somewhat 'down-in-the-dumps' about the impending departure of his family when he arrived on Buccleuch Street to be confronted by a frenzy of activity which seemed to be evolving outside Hank's gym and Star Struck! He started to hasten his footsteps, running more quickly the nearer he approached; and the nearer he approached the more quickly his heart raced, spectators already gathered around began to disperse, recognising Billy and allowing him to get closer.

Billy dropped his small hand luggage at the side of his feet, unable to comprehend the sight before him. Black smoke was smouldering out of the windows of the tenement block where below the burnt-out remnants of Hank's gym and Star Struck, his home and his life as he knew it, faced him.

He made a move to run into the building to find Ivan but he was held back by the baker from across the road, "you're too late lad, they're all away."

What did he mean, 'they're all away'? Did that mean they all managed to get out, unhurt? Oh, the relief he felt for that split second until he saw the five gurneys being wheeled out, each body covered from head to toe, and his head throbbed in bewilderment.

"You'll have t'come t'my place, son," the baker said, placing his arm around Billy's shoulders, "there's nothing left for ye here."

Could his life get any worse than the last few days? He was numb, staring in total disbelief at the horrific destruction in front of him. First it was his mother who had given them all a fright, then the dismaying news of them leaving for America, and now this! It was not possible; it was simply *not* possible! He didn't want to go across the road to the baker's house, he wanted to go to his own home, to Ivan. He wanted to see big Hank's grinning face and tell him it was but a dream, that everything was just as he left, days ago.

His legs buckled underneath him and, unashamedly, he broke down and wailed. He didn't care, he wanted everyone to see how destroyed he was. He was supposed to represent strength and resolve, that's what Hank had taught him throughout his boxing training. *'Never show any weakness, Bill, cos the moment you do, boom – you're down. And when you're down take a second or two to reflect who put you there and why, then look 'em straight in the eye and rise up again slowly, purposefully and finish the job you set out to do'*.

He may have been a fighter, but the fight had left him in those minutes as he watched his past, his present and his future smouldering away like the mist rising above the mountains of the Scottish Highlands on a warm morning.

Gail Preston had heard news of the fire, as had everyone in the vicinity who had come to watch helplessly as the firefighters tried in vain to tackle the blaze, and she knelt silently beside Billy, "your dad's gone Billy, I'm so sorry. Three of the Ralston brothers, and young Mike Healey."

"Mike?" Billy exclaimed in confusion, "what was Mike doing here?"

Gail shook her head, "I dinnae ken."

Emma and Marley had been told the news by Barry Preston after Gail had suggested he would be the best person to break the news to them. He had their telephone number and had spoken to Emma many times during his involvement in the adoption procedures. He reassured Emma that Billy was being cared for by his sister but that he was not in a good state.

In fact Billy was inconsolable, but his demeanour didn't portray grief, it was pure, unadulterated anger and hatred. He was wildly expressing revenge and wanted to pin the blame of the fire onto someone, everyone; a lackadaisical electrician, a careless smoker, anyone - and when he heard that the fire had been started deliberately, he felt murderous!

He tried to reach out to his other two friends, Guy and Joe and wondered why he had seen neither hide nor hair of either of them considering they'd all lost their pal, Mike, in the same tragic nightmare. What kind of friends had *they* turned out to be?

Billy eventually realised exactly what kind of 'friends' they turned out to be when he encountered a very reproachful Guy standing at Edinburgh Station whilst he waited to meet his mum and his sister, with his small brown leather suitcase and wearing his Sunday best standing on the platform for the train bound for London! He was doing a runner!

"Bill, Mike said he was helping you, doing you a favour," Guy spluttered pathetically. "Reckoned you wanted your folk dead, 'specially your dad. We all thought it was strange cos your dad was an ok bloke and folk round here loved him, he was considered something of a hero, brought a lot of the menfolk back. Why did you want him dead?"

Billy was almost speechless, struggling to say his next words, "Ivan was not my *biological* dad, you idiot! He was my Dad, my guardian, my *adopted* dad!!!! Guy, what have you all done?"

The train to London pulled up and Guy climbed aboard, totally dismissing Billy. "I'm glad Mike died in his own creation, and I hope I never see your pitiful face ever again Guy, good riddance and may your demons follow you for an eternity," Billy yelled.

Guy stopped and turned round, "you might want to consider your own demons, Bill."

A lone man of forty or more years sat leaning his head against his crutch on the same platform as the two once-somewhat-friends spat their departing venom. He was nodding and shaking his head at the same time, chuckling like a demented loon. Billy wanted to launch into him; he was stoked, angry and bitter and the last thing he needed at this precise moment was some shell-shocked World War II nutcase mocking him.

"Ivan, did I hear ye mention, the same Ivan that founded the glorious Star Struck on yonder Buccleuch Street, our very own beloved Eiffion Rhys?"

Before Billy could launch into a tirade, he noticed the man had no eyes, only eyelids that appeared fused together. He assumed the man must have been a handsome and muscular able man before he was reduced to this blind, sad excuse for a soldier who was dressed in a shamefully ragged and dirty war-time uniform.

"Eiffion, yes, but likes to be called Ivan now. *Liked* to be called Ivan," he corrected himself.

The blind man laughed heartily. "Aye of course he did, I remember now, he always hated Eiffion," and he continued to sit there sniggering for the longest time.

Chapter 30: The Funeral

Emma and Marley's train was due to arrive in ten minutes' time but Billy was desperate to hear more of the old boy's story, intrigued as to how he knew things about Ivan, or Eiffion as he called him. Everybody in Edinburgh appeared to be more knowledgeable about his Pops than he.

He cursed himself for never asking him any questions about his war service when Ivan had *always* asked Billy about his everyday life experiences and school days, listening intently and encouraging him constantly. Now he no longer had that opportunity, it had disappeared overnight in a blaze of fire. He couldn't even ring Ted to ask his version or opinion. Hindsight – what he wouldn't give for another opportunity to sit and actually talk, to listen and to learn!

He wished he had taken a leaf out of his younger sister's book - she kept a diary and wrote everything inside, the tiniest detail and all her thoughts and aspirations. Billy had no doubt that she would be able to recall many events that he would have totally forgotten about, but he wasn't like that, he hadn't cared that much – then. He did now, though. He tried to search his memory bank for clues, things said… he began to feel something, melancholy perhaps, and as the train screeched to a halt he was overcome with relief as he saw his mum and his adorable, beautiful sister, rising from their seats at the window. He felt safe in the comfort of knowing he was no longer going to handle things alone.

The blind man chuckled again, nodding his head as if he could possibly see and understand what was going on around him. "They bring with them that unforgettable aromatic ambience of Wales that tickle my senses. The abundance of the pink and purple rhododendrons that glorify the mountainous countryside and the hills full of sheep. You understand my drift, young man? I could go on but I have another impending journey to make and I ken you've a journey of your own you'll be making before the new moon rises, so good luck t'yer, lad."

Billy fell into Emma's embrace and turned to look for the blind man as a gesture to introduce his family to him, but he was already gone. He looked up and down the station platform confused to see there was no sign of him.

Gail Preston had offered to accommodate Billy and his family while they collected themselves in readiness for Ivan's funeral. It was going to be an enormous, monumental send off, not only for Ivan but for the three Ralston brothers. Practically the entire population of Fauldhouse was going to be there and a huge gathering of Edinburgh!

Jean Ralston, sister of Hank, Dougal and Davy, was on her honeymoon and Ma Ralston had insisted she stay there; what was the point of dragging her away from wedded bliss to attend the sombre burial of her brothers? She could do her mourning at her own time, as many had had to before – during wartime.

Billy and Emma were totally awestruck as scores of mourners congregated to the kirk, many others standing outside trying to listen to the words of the priest as his voice filtered backwards.

He began by extolling the virtues of the Ralston boys, how all three had admirably fulfilled their duties to Scotland during the war, how they were revered for their deeds in encouraging and nurturing boys from all over into channelling their boisterousness into the gym, thus keeping them off the streets. He hoped their mother would take pride and solace in knowing that her sons were well respected members of the community and prayed that God would continue to bless and comfort her. But Ma Ralston scoffed at his mere words, she could not be comforted, and she walked out of the kirk, laying a hand on each son's coffin before she left.

He then talked of Ivan's bravery, of how so many owed so much to his unselfish actions and how he was respected in and around Edinburgh. Billy had no idea what he was talking about and casually glanced around the congregation to gauge everyone's reactions, he suddenly recognised the dishevelled soldier from the railway station he'd spoken to, leaning on his crutch at the back of the kirk. He raised his hand to wave at him then remembered the old boy was blind and wouldn't be able to see and was therefore surprised when he seemingly smiled back at him, before turning away and disappearing - almost as if in a fog or mist.

Barry Preston shaved that morning, preening himself in the mirror, and splashed on his new cologne that he treated himself to after receiving payment for the all the hard work he had done to secure the legal adoption of Billy and Marley. He and his wife called upon his sister, Gail, to gather to say their goodbyes to the three of them as they began their new odyssey to the United States of America. They were leaving early on Tuesday morning from the train station, eventually arriving at the docks and sailing away.

It was a bittersweet morning and though they should have been overjoyed and excited they were very subdued, particularly Emma and Billy as they reflected on their losses and the numerous memories they would be leaving behind.

Jennifer had not been able to conceal her enthusiasm at finally having her family living close by; she managed to find a nice bungalow for sale, only fifteen miles from where she and Tony lived, in New Jersey. She'd assured them it was perfect for them all, three bedrooms, bathroom (with a shower!), nice big garden, white picket fencing all round so Marley could have her longed-for dog.

She was looking forward to going shopping with her sister, being involved with her niece and nephew's lives, and Tony – who was a huge boxing fan - was looking forward to introducing Billy to the local boxing gym.

The Ryders were quite affluent too; they hosted dinner parties, barbecues, and beetle drives on a regular basis inviting many of their neighbours. They had a television and Jennifer told Emma that everything that happened in the world could be seen and heard in their very own living room.

It all seemed overwhelming for Emma, but America was going to be a brand-new beginning, away from the past and an escape from the possibility of anyone coming to take her children away from her, again.

Emma and Marley had several suitcases each, Billy had just the one, the small one he'd taken to Wales when he visited just days ago. Everything else he had owned and loved had been destroyed in the fire at Star Struck.

He was maturing and had started to grow facial *and* body hair. He needed to ask Emma to buy him a razor once they got to America. He liked the way his body was developing, too. He was tall and muscular, his once copper-ginger hair was now turning a deep auburn and he envisioned getting a tan in this new country in which he was going to live.

He began to imagine himself in a new gym showing off the skills he'd been taught, to these American boxers. He'd dazzle them with the fancy footwork he'd perfected – thanks to all his dancing lessons with the one-and-only Madame Thirlby.

Cassius Clay. That was the name of that good-looking cocky boxer who did a centre-ring jig, enthralling his audience as he smirked in the face of his opponent. He owed it to Hank, Dougal, Davy, and Ivan to be the 'somebody' they all told him he would be, the Benny Lynch gear which had been his prized and most precious possession was now a mere heap of ashes – probably floating around Buccleuch Street, clogging up some drain. But possessions can be replaced, he convinced himself, at least he has memories which no flame can erase. Benny Lynch may have been Scotland's best at the time, but he was going to be bigger and better, stronger and fitter, and only America could put him up there, alongside the best of the best.

The train trundled on. Only twenty more minutes . . . 'I think I can, I think I can, I think I can . . ' He glanced out of the train window, staring at a small patch of yellow rape by the hedgerow and instantly felt nauseas.

Chapter 31: Lillian and Terry

It had felt like déjà vu to Lillian as she sat next to Terry travelling back to Scotland, mourning the absence of her two beloved children, Billy and Marley.

It was so many years ago now since they made that first trip down to Wales. Little Billy had only ever been on one journey before and the momentum of the truck as it bounded along mile after mile, hour after hour had made him travel sick. He vomited on her favourite yellow cardigan, the one it had taken her dear mother two weeks to knit, or so she was told. How could she know? She had never known her mother, she only knew the little snippets she had gleaned over the years, and she still had all her clothes.

She never had understood why Terry had insisted on bringing them all this far after the war ended, but he had reminded her that their father would not be happy to come back home and find more mouths to feed!

Surely not? Wouldn't he be happy to know he was a grandfather and that she was now a mother?

Lillian's simple mind had accepted everything her older brother told her without question, though now she *was* beginning to ask questions – about many things!

She couldn't fathom why she and her babies had had to be locked away, out of sight of the neighbours for one thing; not that they had many neighbours on the Shetland Isles, but Terry assured her that it was all for the best. He wanted to keep them safe from the wickedness of the enemy, the Germans would surely come and kill her and the children because the whole world was fighting and killing each other. The enemy was savage, he'd told her; evil, heartless, and cared nothing for mere women or children.

Terry was a good brother, she concluded. He loved her, took care of her and the bairns, bringing them food, oil for lamps for the long dark nights and many nights he would get into bed with her, snuggling up lovingly, keeping her warm . . .

She just had to keep doing what he told her, stay out of sight and trust no one.

She would get very lonely when he went off to Edinburgh to work at the Apothecary shop, while her father was off fighting the enemy, but on a couple of occasions he had taken her with him and that had coincided with the times Billy and Marley arrived. She chuckled at the memory of Terry telling the prim, elderly lady who helped her with the birthing that she was his cousin - because they didn't have any cousins!

She believed her father must be a great hero because he'd gone to fight the enemy in two wars and he had the battle scars to prove how brave he had been wearing *his* medal over his eye so that everyone would know, and yet she still wondered why this great, powerful, man would be angry with her for allowing his lineage to continue.

Anyway, her father did come back from the war, but he didn't stay long, which was another mystery to Lillian because she knew that the business in Edinburgh had been finished as the entire stock – or what was left of it - was up in their loft along with several bundles of wool that Terry purchased on his last trip to Inverness.

She loved knitting and always had something on the end of her knitting needles. She spent two whole months knitting

Marley's beautiful shawl from the Shetland wool that her mother had kept in her knitting basket - before she was even born. She was proud of that and glad that she had bestowed her daughter something beautiful to wear before they left them both in that barn, in Wales.

Did those people love her children like she did? Would they sing to them like she did? 'Rock a bye Marley on a tree-top, when the wind blows the cradle will rock'. Billy would sing along with her too, his little hand holding on to his baby sister's.

Lilly was none the wiser why her father had suddenly disappeared. Maybe, as Terry explained, he needed time to adjust after all his horrific war memories, meet up with his comrades and enjoy the freedom he had valiantly fought for.

She could almost accept that answer, but she desperately wanted to tell him about his two grandchildren and had begged her brother to bring them back home so she could show them off. She still had some of their toys in the play area Terry had made for them, under the floorboards of their croft.

It wasn't fair, Lilly thought, Terry always did everything his way. And now their dad had left – again, without a word – again, not even helping her brother fill in the 'secret place' underneath the floorboards.

Terry was good at explaining everything to her, but he didn't do a good job of explaining why they were travelling back without their bairns, or why he had hurt the lady when she hadn't done anything wrong. Terry said she had done wrong, though. She'd hidden the babies.

Lillian had missed her babies all those years ago, she enjoyed playing and singing songs with them. "Do you think Marley will be walking yet?" she innocently asked Terry.

"They will be teenagers Lilly," he said, "the lad will most probably be working."

She was confused. How was that possible when he was just a little boy? She tried to picture them both as teenagers, but the very idea was beyond her, remembering them as only wee things and sometimes not very nice things either, always *needing* something, food, the toilet, and those times she found them irritating and would distance herself from them. She liked her dolls in those moments, they were quiet and didn't need feeding.

She stared out of the window as they drove along in silence. She reached into her handbag and took out the lipstick she kept for special occasions, dismayed to acknowledge that it had hardly been used, special occasions being a rarity. She pulled out a compact mirror too and applied the bright red lipstick, going over her lip-line, smiling at herself in the tiny circle of glass and turning to show Terry, "am I still as pretty as picture?" she asked him.

"Always," he replied.

Chapter 32 : The Foundling Siblings - Life in the USA

The bungalow smelled of honeysuckle and Brasso and shone like a bright new pin as Emma packed away all her dusters and polishes, tidying up trying to make everywhere look immaculate. The horse-brasses gleamed around the fireplace and the windows looked to be without glass, they were that clean! Her sister and brother-in-law were coming to stay for the whole weekend to support Billy in his debut professional fight at Madison Square Garden.

Billy had cut the lawn, trimmed the edges, pruned the roses and had even taken the dog out with him for a run that took over two hours. Poor old Beau was exhausted after he got back, taking great gulps of water from the fishpond at the bottom of the garden! He was only three years old and needed loads of exercise - as Border Collies do – more than capable of managing twenty-six miles every day! Billy constantly questioned his sister's inane decision to get another Border Collie rather than the less demanding nature of a Golden Retriever, or a cat! The responsibility of exercising Beau had been placed on him while Marley had to go to school every day, which he didn't mind – really, it was just that the damn dog *had* to be exercised on a daily basis whether he was training or not! Beau didn't have the acres of Trefellon to run wild abandon like Boo had, and a Golden Retriever or a cat would have fitted in with his training regime so much easier.

They had a television now, too, and its arrival had caused much exhilaration. They sat together every evening on the huge sofa debating which channel they were going to watch. Billy's favourite was The Lone Ranger, and he developed a keen interest in Tonto (*Jay Silverheels*), the faithful Indian companion of The Lone Ranger, fascinated by the fact that he was originally born Harold John Smith and that he was an excellent athlete, likening himself that he too was born under a different name and chose a different path in life, admiring his tenacity to break free of the assumed lifestyle of his culture. Marley loved to watch the series too, purely because she adored the character of 'Silver'!

Since Emma had decided to sell up and move to America, she and her twin sister, Jennifer, had managed to rekindle their relationship and once again embraced the close bond they'd enjoyed as children. Jennifer adored her nephew and niece and proved herself to be the 'best auntie in the whole wide world', according to Marley who painted her a certificate with the same words which was framed and hung in the Ryders' kitchen.

Tony, on the other hand, was more taken with Billy. He acknowledged the great upheavals in his young life, the desertion of his parents, moving away to Edinburgh with Ivan, the loss of Ted, and then the unimaginable traumas he went through after losing Ivan and everything in the fire.

He knew, only too well, being an American soldier and having to put on a brave face after learning his best friend and a cousin had been blasted to smithereens during the fateful attack at Pearl Harbor. His lifelong pal, Denzel Barclay, a steward on the USS Virginia, distinguished himself by courageous conduct and devotion to duty, first assisting his mortally wounded comrades before going on to man the machine gun, which he had never operated before, and successfully obliterating an overhead enemy plane. He was awarded the Navy Cross, the service's ultimate award.

His cousin, Judy Donohue, was just thirteen, a civilian living in their small downtown restaurant when a shell struck the building. Tony's aunt and uncle survived, having taken refuge in the basement.

The twin sisters had made plans for the night before Billy's fight and Marley had already demanded Emma buy all the ingredients she needed to bake one of her delicious vegan cakes, notably her favoured date and walnut. Tony was constantly amazed at the similarities between her and his cousin, Judy; always cooking for everyone, always passionate about saving the world and every animal on it. He had no doubt that she would indeed become the vet she had always set her heart on being.

Billy had a new boxing trainer in New Jersey; Jim Knight, and he adored the man! He was so much older than Hank, early-to-mid 70s. He was white-haired, short, and stocky, and he had a broken nose that confirmed it had caught more blows than his handkerchief, but Jim Knight was a gentleman in *every* aspect. He never, ever used bad language, nor did he belittle or ridicule any of his boys. It was as if he was a 'father-figure' to the lot of them, and the respect he gained, not only from the gym and boxing fraternity, but from the local neighbourhoods, too, was evident.

One very ordinary typical Saturday afternoon, Billy had gone off to the shops to buy his monthly boxing magazine, as he did verbatim. Occasionally he would meet up with a gym-buddy or two and discuss the progress of their boxing mentors etc, arguing as to who was the fittest, fastest, finest, and most fascinating, when he passed the barber's shop. He never patronised the barber, hating the 'short-back-and-sides' his mother used to make him sport, he liked his hair long, sometimes falling over his eyes because it was now *very* fashionable, and reminded him of his old stablemate, Norman. Jim Knight suddenly ran out of the barber's shop when he saw Billy walk by the window, his cigarette still burning behind his ear!

"Jim," Billy exclaimed, laughing, "get back inside and let the man finish your haircut before your cigarette burns it all."

He tossed the cigarette away, dismissing Billy's exclamation. "Bill, my hair will grow again before you can say Constantinople and that man will be demanding even more of my dollars. Now then – next Saturday you *have* to be ready, lad. Why are you wasting time here walking idly around when you should be training? This 'Storming Norman' is not a chap you should be taking lightly."

"I've had it drilled into me time and time again 'never underestimate your opponent' and I never have nor ever would," Billy answered, casually.

Jim studied him, smiling "Good, good, because the word out on the grapevine is that it's going to be an explosive revelation."

Billy looked confused as Jim scurried back inside to get the rest of his haircut finished, chuckling at his unique authenticity. He was a character, indeed.

The alarm clocks buzzed at seven o'clock in every bedroom. Marley shot upright, startling Beau who had been sprawled out at the foot of her bed and legged it downstairs to the kitchen where Emma was already sat, traditionally rolling up the crepe bandages that Billy would wrap around his hands before putting on his gloves. They had never been washed in... well, Emma couldn't remember. It was always taboo, to wash the bandages, to wash away the 'luck'. Billy would have had a fit!

Jennifer was the next to walk in, blearily reaching for the cafetiere and opening all the cupboard doors looking for the cheaper quality coffee grains Emma bought rather than the more expensive brand she maintained was more tasteful.

They hadn't long before their taxis arrived, twenty minutes to be precise, and Billy still hadn't made an appearance! He needed to be fed, showered, and changed, packed and ready with no last-minute hitches.

Breakfast was consumed hurriedly, and everyone gathered up their belongings as the taxis beeped their arrival. There were two of them, as Jim and Karl Gunns - his manager - were coming too, naturally to be in his corner.

Billy's first professional fight. He was feeling anxious yet he couldn't fathom why. It wasn't so much as nerves, he couldn't ever recall being nervous before a fight. Only when he stepped under the ropes did the doubts unfold. It was a lonely feeling being there, up in that ring. He was on his own the second that bell rang.

What if he hurt his opponent, or if *he* was hurt? For all that boxing was a gentleman's sport, not all boxers were gentlemen! His family would be there, too, and this compacted on his angst, knowing that they would be on edge, concerned - not only for the results - but that he should come away unscathed.

As he sat in the taxi following the one accommodating his mother, sister, and aunt; he didn't hear the conversation between his uncle, trainer, and manager, only the echo of the words Jim had said the week earlier *'the word out on the grapevine is that it's going to be an explosive revelation'*. What revelation?

Madison Square Garden was not in the least what Billy had expected and his confusion was evident as they drove by, trying to locate the hotel in which they were booked. He'd supposed the building was going to be set in majestic gardens, similar to Princes Street Gardens in Edinburgh, but this was nothing like. More like the library in Inverness, albeit on a much larger and grander scale - it was huge!

He imagined the vast inside and how many people would be coming to watch the many fights, and then he acknowledged that he was now nervous!

Weigh-in was scheduled from three until six p.m. and all boxers were required to check-in with their respective team. Billy decided to explore the surroundings, leaving the hotel and everyone to ooh and ahh at the huge beds, plush carpets, and pristine bed linen. He needed time alone to think about what the coming night would bring. Win or lose, he was still going to get paid, but winning meant the purse would increase with the next fight - and that's what he was in it for - the money! America could provide all the money he needed to recreate Star Struck, provided he kept on winning and dancing to the tune of the elite who paid mega bucks to watch men destroy each other.

It would be bigger, better, more prestigious and notorious than Ivan's Star Struck, and a monument to the man whom he owed so much. He had been imagining it for years and he knew how to do it and where to do it, he just needed the money to set the wheels in motion and boxing - or rather, winning - was going to finance his entire future.

The great doors of Madison Square Garden were opened by two huge, tuxedo-attired African-American bruisers to a ridiculously loud fanfare as the punters confidently entered the foyer searching for the bar where they would spend the next half hour dissecting each and every boxer, placing bets, and professing to know every last detail of the sport before taking their stupidly expensive seats in the hope of leaving much richer than when they arrived.

Billy had bid farewell to his family and he sat in the dressing room with Jim and Karl who were bombarding him with words of encouragement and relaying details of the fights going on in the arena, the atmospheric roars and cheers or boos unable to be heard where they were. His once three two-minute rounds were being replaced with twelve three-minutes' and he had trained for this moment for months. He felt ready, fit, and his adrenalin was pumping as his name was finally called.

He jumped up from the bench he had been sitting on, contemplating the next few minutes and the outcome, and followed his corners.

When he entered the auditorium, he felt his stomach lurch as the spotlights blinded him, cigarette smoke weaving ethereal-like up into the brightness, and the noise from the PA system hurt his ears. He put every thought out of his mind as he stepped into the ring, not even looking around for his family amongst the hundreds already seated. He needed one hundred percent concentration for what he was about to do.

And that was when Jim's words suddenly all became abundantly clear to him. The 'revelation' he hadn't understood now made perfect sense as 'Storming Norman' stepped between the ropes and took off his robe, glancing uncomfortably across to Billy. Norman Morrison!

Billy stared. His mouth gaped open as he gazed at his former stablemate, his considered 'friend' who just upped and left his mother and all those who cared about him without a second thought, and no one had heard another word from him since that day. What the hell was Norman doing in the USA?

Billy turned frantically to Jim, "Jim, I can't fight him! I know him from Edinburgh. We're mates."

"You can't not fight him, Bill. A lot of people have a lot at stake tonight and you *will* fight him."

Billy felt sick. Had Norman known they were going to fight each other? He remembered that he had always known who *his* opponent was going to be. How long had he been here, in America? How long had he been professional? Hundreds of questions buzzed in his mind, and he had no chance of any answers as any second now the bell was going to ring, they would be expected to touch gloves and crack on with what the audience was expecting and had paid for!

'*The word is it's going to be an explosive revelation*'. Who knew? Who had penetrated his mind to be able to comprehend his thoughts?

The referee finished his repartee and summoned both boxers to the centre of the ring, reminding them of the rules and hoping for a good clean fight before sending them back to their respective corners to await the bell. Billy was thinking of things he wished he had said to Norman all those years ago before they were about to meet in the centre and thrash out their differences in front of hundreds of unsuspecting viewers.

'*This isn't Hank's gym in Buccleuch Street, this is Madison Square Garden! We've made it, you and me*', Billy thought to himself.

The bell rang. 'Seconds away, round one'.

The two former friends made brief eye contact as they touched gloves then Billy backed away. This was going to be more than just fighting a matched opponent, this was personal.

They were both tentative for the first minute, appraising one another, both unwilling to initiate the first blow to

315

begin the battle. There was so much that been left unsaid all those years ago when they started training and sparring. Norman wanted to remove his gumshield so that he could talk to Billy to justify himself, explain everything. *'I don't want to fight you Bill, I love you. You can't tell me you didn't know.'*

Marley was ecstatic sitting amongst the fans in Madison Square Garden with her mother, her aunt and uncle, proud to be here to watch her brother win his first professional fight. She had talked non-stop to any of her friends who still cared to show any enthusiasm about boxing, about how her brother was going to be a world-famous boxer. If she wasn't talking about him or her past life in Wales, she was talking about how she was going to become a vet and save all of God's creatures.

Beau had been Marley's Christmas present from Jennifer and Tony for their first Christmas in America after Marley had hinted, embarrassingly so, every time she'd been asked what she would like and whilst Beau was not in the same league as Boo as a proficient sheep dog, he was just as intelligent. He only had to be taught something once and he never forgot as the pair of them entertained family and friends with a little dance routine they'd rehearsed.

Marley had always been the more confident and outgoing of the two siblings. She'd never had the slightest yen to know a thing about her birth parents. To her, Emma and Ted were Mum and Dad, and she loved her new life in America where she felt happy, safe, secure in the knowledge that nothing sinister was lurking in the shadows to whisk her away to God knows where or to what!

She began to alter the way she talked, too, quickly adapting the American dialect so that few recognised her as being an immigrant or a newcomer.

Round three: trivial, almost-pathetic jabs ensued, and the audience began to show their displeasure with raucous heckling, alerting the corners to have serious words with their charges. Jim knew that Billy was more than capable of beating Storming Norman, judging on their past histories, and was dismayed to see that he was under-performing. He needed to find the right words to inject, to get under his skin and make the lad realise his worth and reason for being privileged to share the same ring as the countless other betters.

"Bill," Jim spoke while he poured cold water onto Billy's face as he flopped onto the stool when the bell rang, "I haven't come all this way to stand by and watch a bloody pantomime with two kids straight outta kindergarten, this is a man's world where grudges can be settled. Whatever the gripe between the two of you, get over it now in this ring because if I don't see the real you in the next round, Karl and I will be gone, and you'll have the job of explaining why to your family."

Billy shuffled forwards towards his target and purchased his first meaningful contact, then began pounding and pounding away, body blow after crippling body blow. Tears slowly running down his face as he leaned and pushed his upper body weight forward against Norman's, trying to tire him as he shoved him away in an endeavour to avoid facing him, to not look into his eyes.

Norman eventually retaliated with like-for-like jabs, upper-cuts, body blows, somewhat in shock as he never expected the venom projected from his old pal, as the crowd leapt up on their feet, roaring their appreciation – at last!

The next several rounds were the same, never failing to please the hundreds of spectators who knew – or rather felt - that this fight was going to be the crowd-pleaser it had been rumoured to be.

Billy had never been in a fight lasting for more than the three rounds and was becoming extremely tired. He imagined Ivan, Davy and the others having to fight a war where they were not going to be cheered on or bet against as to who would win, blue corner or red, by those who had nothing better to spend their money on. Ivan *was* the entertainer in every sense of the word, but he was no gladiator, no spectacle of amusement for the ignoramuses of the world. On the contrary he was a hero who had proved that respect, love, and admiration could be earned without the need to destroy.

The bell rang declaring the end of round eleven and both Norman and Billy returned to their respective corners, sweat mixing with the blood that trickled down both of their young faces. One more round to go.

Billy was the first up and he tore across to Norman, landing a superb blow to the stomach, causing him to reel against the ropes as he desperately tried to cover up and catch his breath. The jabs continued and Norman fell. Whatever the adjudicators' score so far, Billy knew that Norman had just lost a point, boosting his confidence. The referee started the count and Norman took his time, remembering Hank's words of encouragement, *'when you're on the floor, take a second or two. Think about who put you there and why. Then, what are you going to do about it?'*

He glared at Billy and inwardly declared war! *He* was going to earn his purse tonight and ensure the punters got their money's worth. He rose quickly and shook himself, wiping the sweat off his brow with his gloved hand, never taking his eyes of Billy who he could see had gained that extra bravado.

Neither boxer could hear the shouting of the spectators as the seconds ticked away on the clock. Billy decided to mock his opponent with fancy footwork, hoping to distract him, but Norman was storming, and a left uppercut put Billy on his bum! The crowd roared louder, and then the bell rang. It was done.

Norman looked over to Billy, confused as to why he spat out his gumshield into the bucket aside his stool, and then gesticulated to his trainer to untie his gloves. It was almost Déjà vu as he remembered Hank's laugh *'bare knuckling boxing went out with the Ark, Bill, get' em back on,'* and Billy winking, saying to Norman, *'see you in ten minutes – max'*.

Un-gloved, Billy walked to join Norman and the referee in the centre of the ring, grabbed his hand and raised it in the air, pronouncing him the winner . . but the judges had scored differently – it was a tie! The scorecards were identical.

The turning point in their lives came about because of history and destiny. The boys had become men who never acknowledged their adolescent feelings for each other, until now. Neither oceans nor years could alter their fate, and they left the ring unanimous.

A 'revelation' indeed!

Epilogue: The Battlefield

The noise of the battlefield was indescribable. The sight, the sound, the smell of fear and death never went away, morning, noon, or night; for ever. It was agonising to wake up in the morning and realise that you were still alive and would have to go out to fight another cruel and lonely day. Men cried like babies and trembled for hours until they were eventually overcome with exhaustion and somehow managed to close their weary eyes in sleep, for however long the good Lord allowed.

None of them had the slightest clue of what it was going to be like when they were either called-up or enlisted. How could they? Especially those who had never been at war before - those first timers. The ones who had been in the first war were under no illusion as to what to expect but it hadn't made it any easier at all! In fact, most considered the chances of returning home in one piece, or if at all, were practically zero!

Hundreds of letters to loved ones were written on scraps of paper using worn-down pencils, every one of them omitting descriptions of the unthinkable circumstances that every single soldier encountered day after day after day; simple messages were painstakingly concocted to avoid the reader knowing the truth of what each and every one of them endured because the reality was too unreal to write about, too grotesque.

Ivan was glad that he had Davy by his side. They'd all enlisted together, swearing to look after each other; Ivan, Davy, and James. How they had admired themselves in their pristine uniforms, boots polished to a perfect shine, cheerfully confident as they marched off to join the ranks of others, apprehensively excited at sailing away to foreign lands in an endeavour to win the war and defend their King and Country.

James was the youngest of the trio at just seventeen years old. He was the only remaining son of May and Johnny Rogers, his two other brothers losing their lives in the First World War. Blond-haired, blue-eyed James had wanted to follow in his older brother's footsteps and join the Navy but after George lost his life along with almost two thousand others when his ship, the RMS Lusitania, a passenger liner, was torpedoed and sank off the Old Head of Kinsale in Ireland, May had pleaded with him to reconsider. The thought of their youngest, and now only son, being at sea and at war, was too much for her and Johnny to bear.

George was already in the Royal Navy when WW I broke out, so his enlistment had been a mere formality. John Jr was a pilot in the Royal Air Force. May Rogers received two telegrams on the same morning informing them, albeit cruelly and unsympathetically, that both of her beloved, handsome, and charismatic sons were 'missing in action' and as the deliverer of this devasting news turned on his bicycle to ride away to continue his route of destruction, she fell to her knees, howling like a banshee.

Never in a million years did May and Johnny expect history to repeat itself only a few years later whereby yet another son was commandeered to do his duty, and with having previously lost two sons in the air and at sea, she had finally managed to persuade James to enlist as a soldier.

His expertise with the rifle had not gone unnoticed and he felt a great sense of achievement when he was described as one of the finest snipers to ever come out of Edinburgh. Ivan hated the thought of shooting anything or anyone and James had initially felt the same way - until he made his debut kill.

Ivan had needed to relieve himself. Dysentery was rife and everybody always tried to move as far away from their comrades as possible when it came to finding somewhere to squat that was going to cause the least offense! As Ivan rushed to the undergrowth and took down his trousers, James spotted a moustached German soldier take up his rifle and aim at his friend. He didn't even take a second to consider his alternatives because to James, there was none, it was either the German or it was Ivan, and the next miniscule of a second Ivan found himself being showered in a hot, wet liquid all over his back. He turned around to see the practically headless German fall backwards where he remained lifeless for an eternity and if Ivan had felt any loosening of his bowels, seconds before, he certainly didn't now as the entire contents of his whole being was dispelled behind that clump of foliage!

He owed his life to James who was proving himself everyday out there in the pits of hell, ending the lives of young men in the same situation as themselves who would also be sending the same prayers to keep them safe to the very same God as the thousands alike.

Who *was* this great and wondrous God going to listen to and grant salvation? Who *did* God consider worthy saving opposed to those who were not? Was it random selection or was it all preordained? Many asked if indeed there was such a loving, caring Deity; one who was supposed to hear everyone's prayers and forgive all sins yet appeared to have forsaken His whole brethren out there on those bloodied, bastardised killing fields and beyond.

Ivan no longer knelt in prayer, he considered religion a farce, having decided the only people he could totally rely on were his friends and comrades, and, likewise, he vowed to do his utmost to protect them, even though many miracles were witnessed all the time.

Be damned to King and Country; he vowed to himself he would not kill, ever. He would not have another man's blood on his conscience to haunt him for evermore like the time he killed the lone rabbit to satiate his hunger that day whilst walking to Edinburgh. No! Enough.

He wouldn't tell a soul about the decision he'd made; he would have been ridiculed and tormented unforgivingly like that obnoxious, cowardly character William 'Patch' Irving, who everybody loathed.

And so . . Ivan Rhys changed strategies, rather than be a killer, he decided he was going to be a saver, but not like the medics they had, no.

He didn't sleep that night as he began to plan exactly the structure he had spinning in his mind. He snuggled up closer to Davy who was already snuggled up close to James on the external pretence of maintaining body warmth but in fact was not the entire truth he acquiesced as his hand reached down to Davy's that was already linked with James' and for the first time in a long time, they all slept . . . until being awakened by the unmistakable sound of gunshots, reminding them of another precipice of a journey into damnation.

It was noon, Saturday, 1 July 1945 and it was Hank's birthday. Davy had colluded with his brother, Dougal, and his friends, Ivan and James, to try and conjure up the most embarrassing way possible during these extreme times to celebrate Hank's big three O birthday! Everyone was hoping and praying there would be some calm so that they could have something substantial to celebrate to take their minds away from the inevitable forthcomings, and it seemed that at long last, their prayers had been answered, for a moment. News had been banded around the troops that the German forces were bending under the weight of intensive bombing by the Brits causing them to retreat east, lessening their manpower slightly. It was uplifting for everyone; it gave them an element of hope for some reprieve.

Ivan, Davy, and James had planned to entertain their comrades with a rendition they used to perform at The Swinging Sporran back in the days before being transported into hell. They danced and sang to a little routine they had concocted; it was comical too and all three thought this was the perfect birthday surprise. It was also a dead cert that Hank would be mortified... Wonderful!

The three friends stripped down to their underwear - grubby as it was - it mattered not. Their skinny, white torsos and legs looked hilarious in their thick socks and well-worn boots as they began their act. Wolf-whistles were screeching in abundance, the clapping of hands and stomping of feet by an exhilarated audience ensued as the three began to sing and dance in front of a very miffed and hugely embarrassed Hank! He leapt up from his sitting position to confront Ivan just as an overhead German plane unloaded its deadly cargo, causing everyone to scatter amid the squeals and booms all around.

James was one of the first casualties of those first few seconds, his almost-skeletal body was unrecognisable as a man, with hardly any limb remaining. A writhing mass of blood and guts replaced the once youthful and laughing third and only remaining son of May and Johnny.

Davy instinctively fell to his side, trying pathetically and hopelessly to get his friend to reassure him that he was ok.

Everybody was screaming, scattering, and running for cover but Davy had remained by his friend's side, seemingly oblivious to the surrounding mayhem and the fact that he now had blood running down his chest from his shoulder.

Ivan, who had been running away to the sparse salvation of shrubbery, realised his two pals were not with him and he turned to watch Davy, bleeding, and cradling the splattered remains of James.

The enemy was now advancing towards them, and he could do nothing to save either of them. He panicked. He could not lose them. They came into this war together and they would leave or die together, and he didn't want to die without letting Davy know just how much he loved him.

He was the first person he'd ever felt liberated with. Though he and Davy had shared many conversations and hours, they had a comforting connection, a knowing that didn't need explanation. Davy's two brothers didn't have a clue, and they certainly wouldn't welcome Ivan with open arms if they had any inkling of how he felt for their young brother! On the contrary, friend or foe, Ivan would be dead meat!

Blasts of gunshots bombarded over the ensuring hours. Another plane flew low overhead, bullets finding their targets as one after another bit the dust, their agonising screams embedded in the memories of their colleagues, which would eventually haunt them for their entireties.

Ivan had still not fired a single shot. His two friends lay out there, ten, twenty, thirty yards away, dying, wounded and alone, but he would not retaliate, even though he felt murderous.

Hank told Dougal to back him as he was going to go out to bring Davy back, but Dougal insisted on joining him. "Dougal," Hank said, "Ma needs us all back, stay here with the Nancy-boy and just make sure you don't miss. If you see one of them German bar-stewards take aim and kill the bastard, let Mrs Krauts do some grieving instead." As he took his first two steps towards his younger brother, a flying bullet from behind took off the top of his ear, blood spurting all over his face and into his eyes, his hands tried desperately to wipe it away so that he could see his way to reach Davy.

Night-time fell all too quickly, and the remaining men were despondent, sickened, wounded and petrified. Ivan lay on his belly and crawled out under the darkness towards where he knew his friends lay, one definitely dead, the other dead or injured. He first encountered Hank and grabbed him by his arm, "Hank, I'll get Davy, let's get you back first. You look ok, just lost a bit of your ear but I think I can safely say 'you'll die after it'", he chuckled.

Hank crawled back with Ivan, like a couple of slithering snakes. When Hank was back in a safe zone, Ivan returned to fetch Davy. It was eerily silent, bar the groans and murmurs of the wounded.

Davy was lying next to what was left of James, his bloodied hand on the gaping hole of their friend's chest. He seemed unresponsive as Ivan whispered his name, so he began to pull him away, a dead weight, slowly, inch by inch.

A German sniper had been biding his time as he watched Ivan trying to prise Davy away from James and as he fell backwards, he felt an excruciating pain in his knee knowing that he'd taken a hit. He was even more determined to get his friend back to safety and the administration of the medical staff.

With Hank and Davy now safely back outside the line of fire, Ivan, dismissing his pain, returned to the countless other wounded and dying within everyone's vision and hearing.

Thirteen men he recovered from the battlefield that night. Thirteen men who would have otherwise perished out there without the intervention of any medical assistance. Some of their wounds were horrific with missing limbs, bullets embedded in their bodies, ears bleeding from the intensity of the blasts and force of the bombs being dropped around.

Ivan had point-blank refused any help with his injury while he steadfastly ignored his pain and pursued his plight to bring their wounded comrades back to their side.

He took one last look at what had once been his friend, James. He remembered the story he told of his brothers during the First World War and of his mother's wish that he didn't follow in their footsteps, urging him to become a solider instead. He made a promise to himself that he would visit James' parents - if he managed to return from this nightmare alive - and tell them what a hero their son was, they could be proud. But May and Johnny had heard it all before, twice before, and any feeling of pride would come nowhere near the feeling of grief, loss, despair, and bitterness.

Hank and Davy's wounds were superficial, Ivan's was more substantial, which resulted in his war effort conclusion. He not only lost his leg but one of his dearest friends – as did numerous others, of course - and he also wondered if he would ever again feel the same enthusiasm for life.

Ivan sank into a deep depression during his months of convalescence, overwhelmed with a perpetual feeling of shame and guilt at being back in Civvy Street when he thought about the millions of others who were not as fortunate as he. Those brave and still-able souls out there on those bloody killing fields who he knew would be sending up the same daily, unanswered, prayers to an absent God as they awakened each morning to endure another grotesque and hideous day.

What was it all about? Why did so many have to forfeit so much for something all too pointless?

His little piece of metal on a fancy-coloured ribbon proffered by a person of notoriety who had not the slightest idea of what it felt like to shit yourself in the face of utter fear and dread losing all dignity, was totally insignificant, whatever regal name it was given.

He didn't feel proud at all. He didn't consider himself a hero, in fact he felt a little insulted by the commendation - it was just a 'medal' - and Ivan felt that every single participant of every single war merited the title of 'hero'.

He tossed it in the bin aside his now empty hospital bed, along with the Bible, and painkillers he was no longer in any need of. He picked up the crutch he'd been given, said his goodbyes to all around and embraced a new daylight.

Davy, Dougal, and Hank were waiting outside. It was time to go home.

Just a Little Insight Into the Future ...

The grand opening of 'The Turning Point' was happening this very night! Bill and Norm had been running around frantically like a couple of headless chickens for the last few weeks, ensuring that everything was going according to plan. They'd packed in their boxing careers (careers? Ha!) two and half years ago and 'The Turning Point' was their very own creation, a brand-new beginning, similar theme to Star Struck but on a bigger and much grander scale.

They'd upped sticks and moved to San Francisco where their union was totally acceptable and their new venture was a foregone conclusion to bring forth unspeakable dollars, thanks to the legacy of Tony who passed away two months after the debacle at Madison Square Gardens. Tony had bequeathed Billy thousands of dollars and Jennifer had purchased a modest ranch only thirty miles away from them after she sold up in New Jersey, all in Marley's name! Two exceptionally large 'grannie-flats' had been erected on the periphery of the estate for her and her sister to live out their dotage together.

She was about to graduate from college and go on to study veterinary care, which was befitting seeing as though she had now acquired two more dogs, a pony, four sheep, three cats, a rescued donkey, two goats and twelve chickens!

She never, ever did find a haggis!

Acknowledgements

Being a writer gives one an immense feeling of satisfaction and fun, especially when it's all finished and published with a nice front cover, and it gets out there to willing readers.

For me, I feel it's akin to doing a jigsaw puzzle. You do the outside first to form the structure, then you fill in the middle. Or alternatively, like baking a cake you haven't tried before. You have an idea what you want to make and gather all the necessary ingredients. You weigh them, sort them, then start adding them into a bowl, gradually adding more and more ingredients, stirring everything as you go along, tasting a little from time to time. When you have the consistency you feel satisfied with, you cook it, remove it from the oven and decorate it as befitting as you like.

Next, you have the worrying ordeal as you serve it out, anxiously waiting for the inevitable feedback!

I am incredibly fortunate to have a superb team on my side. My wonderful and amazing sister, Carolyn Irving, and my fabulous friend, Karen Tyres, who painstakingly plough through every word, checking and altering my many mistakes. My exceptionally youthful 90-year-old mother, Elizabeth Talbott, who reads everything I write to ensure I'm on the right path and would have my 'guts for garters' if I wrote anything profoundly inappropriate for her eyes or indeed those of my nieces and nephews. My two readers, Suzanne Bottomley and Patricia White, whose opinions I value as to the authenticity and entertainment value.

And then there's Mike Hurd – my publisher (Lineage Independent Publishing) - whom I've never met face-to-face as we live oceans apart. There's a lot to be said for trust and respect. I'm sure there was much of that on the battlefields I mentioned when describing Ivan's heroics during the war, having someone to watch out for you, trusting them implicitly. The same can be said of a boxing trainer or manager, like Billy had, matching him against an equally proficient opponent. Mike has had the same ultimate faith in me, producing this and my previous two other books. Without him, there would be no Weep and Wail, or Spud, or A Patch of Yellow. I'm forever in your debt, Mike.

A Patch of Yellow is purely fictional and certain historical events have been written for entertainment purposes only, and not to be misinterpreted as fact.

Other Works by Lisa Talbott:

Pen and Inks (Kindle and paperback), with illustrations by Lucas Volaart-Vermeulen

Weep and Wail (paperback and e-book), with Michael Paul Hurd

Spud (everything is meant to be) (paperback and e-book)

Lightning Source UK Ltd.
Milton Keynes UK
UKHW010636090522
402703UK00001B/59

9 781087 976273